Miss Classified

Susan Phelan

To The Burgham family — You guys are loved — all of you — every piece. Susan Phelan

CHICKEN SCRATCH BOOKS
WWW.CHICKENSCRATCHBOOKS.COM

Chicken Scratch Books
PO Box 104
Wisdom, MT 59761

www.chickenscratchbooks.com

Publisher's Note: This is a work of fiction. Names, characters, places, and
incidents are a product of the author's imagination. Locales and public names
are sometimes used for atmospheric purposes. Any resemblance to actual
people, living or dead, or to businesses, companies, events, institutions, or
locales is completely coincidental.

Ordering Information: Special discounts are available on quantity purchases
by corporations, associations, and others. For details, contact the publisher at
the address above.

First Chicken Scratch Books Printing, 2022

ISBN 978-1-953743-16-9 (paperback)

ISBN 978-1-953743-17-6 (ebook)

Printed in the United States of America

To my family for putting up with my dreams
and
To all those who are struggling with brain issues
that often seem to make life hard, but sometimes
make life magical.

Chapter 1
Tuesday Night

The Funeral

I lead the solemn procession to the graveyard in the back corner by the empty house next door. As I'm now thirteen, Mom says I can take charge, which has my hands shaking a little. I need to get this right.

Funerals are important.

My hands are empty except for a small shovel I carry for the job ahead. I grip the handle tight, so the shaking won't make me drop it.

"Here lies Vlad the dwarf hamster, Dobbin the hermit crab, and the ashes of our dog, Benny," I say soberly while we walk. Benny ran out the front door when I was five and got hit by a car. I remember taking naps on his stomach and curling my fingers in his soft fur to fall asleep. And I remember how his funeral made me happy and sad at the same time, like my heart was broken but the funeral taped it together so it could heal. I want Mason and Sarah to feel that. "Now we'll add Lester the lizard."

Mason walks slowly behind me. I hear him sniffling. Which is expected. It was his lizard. Sarah is behind him, jumping on the few dead leaves on the ground. It's only September, so the crunch isn't loud.

When we reach the graveyard, I move to the side, so Mason and Sarah can stand beside me.

"He needs a coffin," Mason says through his sniffles. He holds Lester out in front of him in his cupped hands. Lester isn't a very big lizard, but at six, Mason's hands aren't very big either, and Lester's tail sticks out over the end of Mason's hands.

Sarah runs back to the walnut tree and grabs two giant leaves from the ground. She's only four, but a fast thinker. "We can make him a bed," she says.

Mason nods. I grab one leaf from Sarah, lay it on the ground, and take Lester. He feels cool and rough. I rub my finger over his bumpy back for the last time and set him down on the leaf. It's lucky Lester died nice and straight so he fit well. I don't think Mason would be happy if Lester were hanging off the side of the leaf. I take the other leaf and fold down the first few inches, ripping off the top part. This makes a nice blanket.

I drop the little broken part and we watch it flutter to the ground.

Sarah picks it up. "This can be his pillow." She slips it under Lester's head. "He looks like he's sleeping."

Mason nods again, takes the shovel from me, and starts digging.

*****

2

Getting ready for bed, I notice a light zipping around outside my window. I look out and see Dad with his arm around Mason, by the graveyard. Mason's shoulders are slumped and his hand comes up and wipes his face.

I think about running down there to be with them, but it looks so peaceful I don't want to disturb things. I step to the door of my room, where my backpack is sitting, pull Polly, my Polaroid camera, from her pocket, and slip back to the window.

Mason bends down and puts something by the grave. Dad shines the flashlight on it and I can see that it's a grave marker made from Popsicle sticks. Mason walks away a few steps, but Dad bends down, sets the flashlight by the marker, and moves the marker around until he seems happy with where it is.

Dad will want it to be perfect, like everything else he does.

He picks up the flashlight, takes Mason's hand, and they walk back to the house.

Before they can get far, I pull Polly up to see what she thinks, but I can tell it's too dark, even with the flashlight, to get a very good picture. I'll have to freeze-frame this in my mind to remember it forever.

I yawn as I put Polly away and notice my math book open with a blank sheet of paper and a number two pencil next to it where I left it before the funeral. I yawn again. I think Ms. Carter should accept a funeral as an excuse for not getting my math homework done.

Chapter 2
Wednesday Morning

When It Dawned On Me

Late again. I sprint out the front door of the house and freeze when I see Dad standing *inside* the school bus. Mom runs down the front lawn in her fuzzy, red bathrobe, her arms waving, looking like a bullfighter taunting a giant, yellow bull. She must see Dad inside the bus because she stops running and heads back toward the house.

"Please, Mom. Go inside before a camera crew comes," I say, shivering at the thought.

Mom climbs the stairs as I hurry down. She holds her hand up for a high five, but I ignore her. With my backpack on one shoulder and my toast in hand, I jump over my brother's skateboard on the last step, run into the street, and fly up the bus steps. Dad lectures Asteroid (better than calling him Zit Man), the driver about something, and I try to squeeze behind Dad to find a seat on the bus, hoping no one will know this guy in the tweed coat belongs to me. He could be some random guy, right?

Nope. He has to make things worse.

"There she is—Blythe, my future brain surgeon. She'll be supporting our retirement with her income. Do you know she's in the 99th percentile on last year's national placement tests?" Dad says, giving me a wink. "Jacob here was a student in my physics class last year," he says to me, pointing at Asteroid.

Dad expects me to smile, so I do, but my heart is beating hard and I'm sure the kids in the front can hear it over the bus's engine.

It's bad enough Dad thinks I'm smart, now everyone on the bus knows he thinks I'm smart.

Again I try to push past Dad.

Asteroid looks down, his hand on the door shifter thing and Dad looks down too.

"I suppose I should let you get on with your route," Dad says, stepping back a bit.

Anxious to get away before Dad keeps talking about me and my brains, I scrabble past him. He shuffles my hair as I pass, and I swallow a scream.

As he walks to our house, Asteroid closes the bus door and turns up the Rock and Roll music, or some other kind of old stuff.

"Bly is on the fly again!" He yells. "You've got the coolest dad."

Please stop. I give my tight smile again and say, "How come the bus is so empty?"

Asteroid turns the music down. "Field trip."

"Oh, yeah." At least there are fewer people to see my

humiliation dressed in a fuzzy, red bathrobe and a professor's suit, complete with patches on the elbows.

My seat is empty so I plop down—fourth row back, left side. The eighth-grader on the other side of the aisle has her head down in her phone.

I'd asked for a phone but Dad said, "Ain't happening, kid." I might be the only seventh grader without one. But Dad did give me Polly, and I wouldn't trade her for a phone.

I sit, put my feet up on the seat next to me, and lean back. I munch my cold toast making sure the crumbs land on my backpack. Some butter sticks to my lips and I lick it off.

Something stinks like bubble gum and flowers and I cover my nose.

I scoop the crumbs onto my napkin with my other hand and stuff it into my back pocket. Then I pull my lip-gloss out of the small pocket in my backpack.

Wait. Backpack. School.

No. No. No.

Dumping the contents of my backpack on the seat, I scan through everything.

It isn't there. I did a few math problems last night after watching Mason and Dad. Did I leave it in my room?

I fumble through the pile. Four books, my photography magazine, three crumbled scratch papers, and something that looks like it's for sewing class.

My brow is wet and I wipe my hand over it, dampening the edges of my hair. "Oh, crumb bum. I've done it again."

No one seems to hear me, including Asteroid, who's

bouncing in his seat to some song that tells him to "get down."

Turning in my seat to the window, I do a calculation, using my lip-gloss like a pencil on the glass. Twelve math assignments, zeros on nine of them. That's 25%. Even with a perfect test score last week, I'm doomed. Three weeks into the school year and this toast had popped. Like my dad's eyes would pop when he saw my grades.

My breathing speeds up like I'm running late to class. My chest hurts and I squeeze my fists over my eyes and push, trying to stop the tears. I count backward by sevens starting at 103.

103, 96, 89, 82, 75.

My breathing slows a bit and I drop my hands. I have to think this through. Everything has an answer. I just don't know what it is yet.

Something is wrong and I have to figure out why nothing I try works for seventh grade. Teachers expect homework when it's due and they expect me to be listening all the time. They expect me to remember what they expect.

How do I tell Dad? I shudder and put my head between my knees, knowing my excuses don't work this year.

I bite some of the cherry flavor off as I chew on my bottom lip, hoping somehow the homework will appear in my hands. But of course, it doesn't. Magic only works in books.

Before my eyes decide to fill again, I pull out my napkin from breakfast to wipe off the window. Then I shove the napkin back into my pocket so hard, I feel a small rip in the seam.

Sarah would call this day stinky. And she'd be right. Like the smell I keep almost gagging on.

A girl in front of me turns around. "Is my perfume bothering you? I kind of spilled it as I was putting it on." That's what the bubble gum flower mix must be.

"No, it's fine," I say. It isn't, but I try to be nice.

A paper airplane flies overhead bringing more perfume smell with it and I think my toast might come back up. I open the window a crack and put my nose out, reaching for fresh air.

The sky has cleared a little from the night's rain but heavy cotton ball clouds still shift with the breeze against a hazy blue. Some of the clouds have blue-grey bottoms. The kind that can roll together into a giant mass and hurl rain down so hard and fast you get soaked running from the bus into the school.

My fingers take the shape of Polly's viewfinder and I stare into the sky from behind the rectangle. If only I could fly into those clouds and snap pictures close up. Those would look cool.

Behind me I hear some boys hooting like it's a football game.

"And here come the cheerleaders, just in time," I whisper. My shoulders slump, knowing what's coming.

The bus stops by Stanley's Corn Stand where some kids are waiting. The corn stalks behind them are taller than the tallest kid. The breeze has the corn silks blowing back like a hair commercial.

Cherie gets on the bus, chatting with her friend. Both

wear their cheerleading skirts and the hooting from the back morphs into cheers. Cherie beams her perfect smile and waves her perfect wave as she works her way down the aisle. Her straight blond hair swishes back and forth like the corn silks outside. "Hey, Sondra, cute hair. Tim, you're on the football team? Love how you look in the jersey. I'll be cheering for you."

I shake my head, disgusted at how fake she is.

When she gets to me, she gives a quick look of smelling something gross. Then she plops down in the seat behind me.

I wish Porter sat with me, instead of being on a field trip. Maybe then that look of hers wouldn't make me feel like I swallowed a piece of wood. Porter would get me thinking of something besides Fake Girl.

But I'm stuck today.

Alone.

I swallow, trying to make the feeling in my throat go away.

"So, did you watch 'TV Sensations' last night? I can't believe they think Vince Shropshire is hotter than Mike Samson," I hear Cherie say.

Her friend answers something I can't hear and Cherie says, "Yeah, when my band gets on 'TV Sensations' we'll blow everyone away. Daddy bought me some light-up drumsticks. They're so fine. Here's Vince's song."

Pieces of drums and lyrics hit my ears, but I tire of listening, and sink lower in my seat, staring at the weave in the back cushion cover.

I pull Polly from the side pocket of my backpack and angle her so the light from the window shines through onto the weave. I'm close enough that you can't tell what you're seeing, but it looks really cool. I snap the picture, wait for the photo to zip from the bottom of the camera, and then pull it out. I put Polly back in her safe place and slip my math book from my backpack.

How many math problems can I get done before the picture develops?

Chapter 3
Wednesday School

Sew What?

By the time we get off the bus, I have five of eleven problems done, but I know Ms. Carter won't be happy. Pink marker on the crumpled back of my sewing class paper will get points docked.

But I'm excited about my picture. It turns out super cool. It kinda looks like sand dunes at sunset. I hold it in my hand so it won't get messed up in my backpack.

I can't stop looking at it.

I'm almost to the school door when someone bumps my shoulder. The picture flies out of my hand and flutters to the ground.

"No," I shout. I dive into a mass of legs and feet. Crawling over the rough concrete, I hope to grab the picture before it gets stepped on or pushed into the muddy spot that's always next to the door.

"Hey."

"Watch out!"

Someone falls on top of me and my arms give out, landing my chin on the concrete. I lay there, trying to catch my breath when someone trips on me and a knee lands in the middle of my back, making me lose the bit of breath I've caught. The photo is inches from my fingers and hanging over the side of the concrete entry. My chin feels like a dentist's drill is buzzing into it. I grit my teeth and concentrate on touching the photo. A slight breeze and it'll land in the mud. My fingers almost grab it when a hand, with perfectly manicured nails, reaches down and lifts it beyond my reach.

The last of the feet stomp off and I rise as fast as I can. Which isn't very fast, as my whole body aches. Cherie stands there, holding my picture with the tips of her fingers, like it's contaminated. She reaches her hand out to me.

"Is this yours?"

I nod.

She opens her thumb and finger and the picture sails to the ground. "Oops," she says as she saunters off.

As she walks away, I hear her whisper under her breath. "Weirdo."

The first bell rings overhead, and I cover my ears. When it stops, I slide down the wall until I'm sitting against the building and grab the picture from the edge of the puddle. The corner of the picture needs a wipe, so I use the bottom of my shirt, being as careful as I can.

I will not let Cherie ruin my day.

I hold the picture to my chest, close my eyes, and tell myself to breathe. I just need a minute to calm down. Taking the napkin from my pocket, I give it a shake and watch the toast crumbs fall to the ground. I find a clean spot on the napkin and wipe the drips from my nose and eyes. My body hurts and so do my feelings, but I can do this. I take another deep breath. This one is less shaky than the last.

The late bell rings and when it stops I pull myself up to a stand, and again stuff my multi-use napkin into my back pocket. Taking one more deep breath, I square my shoulders, pull open the door, and march inside.

I stop in the office to get a late pass and a bandage for my chin, and head to my locker. After stashing my picture safely away on the locker's top shelf, I walk into Mrs. Brimhall's room.

The humming of the sewing machines hits me before I grab the doorknob and I can feel my brain fighting the sound. Most everyone inside has their eyes down either cutting material, sewing it, or picking out mistakes. My machine sits empty, waiting for me. . . except I don't have my material yet.

When I get home, I'll tell Mom we need to go to the store. I'm sure I'll remember this time. I tear off a small corner of my late note from the office to write myself a reminder, then stuff the reminder in my back pocket with the napkin.

I hand Mrs. Brimhall the rest of the late note. She's super tall and my head only comes to the chain dangling from her neck. It holds bunches of things, including her glasses, a pencil pull, and a tiny pair of gold scissors covered with black etching.

"Oh, my, Blythe," she says. "What happened to you?"

I touch my chin and wince. "I, um, fell on my way into

school."

"Oh, you poor dear. Well, here. I've got a new comb in my top drawer. Go across the hall, comb your hair, and wash up a bit."

Comb in hand, I run across the hall to the bathroom. No wonder Mrs. Brimhall looked at me like I'd crawled out from some hole in the ground. My clothes are covered in dirt and my hair looks like it doesn't know what a comb is. I have brown streaks on my face and my elbow is skinned. That's why it burns. A tear escapes my left eye but I brush it away.

"I said I wouldn't let this ruin my day. And I won't." I stand straighter and take a deep breath. I just need a minute to calm down. My body and feelings may hurt but I'll get over it. My picture is safe and that's what counts.

I say it out loud to help me believe it. Looking in the mirror I repeat, "My picture is safe and that's what counts."

When I've cleaned up, I go back to the room and sit. With no material, I'm not sure what to do, so I watch everyone, the machine humming twirling in my brain. Our class is all girls. Some boy came the first day, but I never saw him again.

What happened to him?

The machine humming takes over my brain and I see the story in my head.

NEWS ANCHOR: In other news, we have a story from Champaign, Illinois about a young man, missing for six years, who has been found. Here's our correspondent.

CORRESPONDENT: I'm standing by the house of a local

resident, talking to a man who has been missing since he was fourteen. He just climbed out of this storm cellar. Tell me, young man, what is that in your arms?

YOUNG MAN: Prom dresses.

CORRESPONDENT: And why were you in the storm cellar?

YOUNG MAN: When I went to sewing class in Junior High, I was the only boy. I didn't want anyone to laugh at me, so I stayed in the storm cellar until I could prove myself.

I giggle, then stand and walk around the classroom. A new poster on the wall catches my eye. It looks familiar. I slip back to my seat and pull out my dog-eared photography magazine. A flip or two and I find it. The poster is the same picture as in my magazine, by my favorite photographer, Jennifer Gardoney, except the poster has words: "Dare to do, Dare to be" against rolling sand dunes.

I'll have to compare it to this morning's picture to see if mine really looks like sand dunes.

The only thing alive in Ms. Gardoney's picture is a bird sitting on a stick. When I look at it, I feel like I'm the bird, about to fly off, if I could only decide which direction I want to go.

I don't feel like I can sit. The ick in my stomach from Cherie's meanness is still there, so I wander around again. I pass Marsha Hickock, her hair in its usual long braid down her back. The clothes she wears look like maybe her grandma wore them when she was a girl. But her pajama material is cute. It's full of little flowers in blue and white.

"I like your material," I say, reaching out to feel it. "Where did you get it?"

Marsha stops sewing and looks somewhere around my shoulder when she answers. "Cotton Giant. Thanks." She ducks her head and goes back to sewing.

A few people hide their phones as I pass.

I walk the rest of the way around the room and hear a voice.

"Blythe, may I help you?"

Looking up at Mrs. Brimhall's long face, her nose pointed down at me, my brain freezes and my heart pounds. Was she going to yell at me? "Um. Yeah. I. . . oh. Sorry. Sometimes the sewing machine noise spaces me out. Um, I wanted to get the list of stuff we need for the next project."

That sounds good so I go with it.

"I haven't seen you working on your pajama pants. Is everything okay?"

"Yeah, I, um. . . sorry."

I scoot to my seat before she can ask me anything else.

The girl next to me piles her sewing scraps on the table. They're tiny strips of pink, with green and purple dots. The way they're piled looks like an ice cream sundae, so I pull out Polly to see what she thinks. I move around until we see nothing but fabric. The sun glints off one of the pieces on top. Bam! Got it.

As the camera whirs out the picture, Mrs. Brimhall turns.

"Oh, crumb bum," I say to myself. I hold Polly under the

table and look innocent.

A click, click, click sound slides under the whir of the machines and Mrs. Brimhall's pointy heels are soon in front of me. I look way up to see her face. She bends over and her dangling chain swings right in front of me. "Blythe, you didn't answer my question before. I don't see you working. Is everything okay?"

My stomach starts the thing it always does when I get caught. Kind of a twisty, tingly, throw-up feeling. I do the only thing I know to do—make something up.

"I guess not, Mrs. Brimhall. I don't feel well." My stomach is churning, so I'm not lying.

"Why don't you put your head down for the rest of class? But, pajama pants are due soon, so I suggest you do some of your work at home."

"Yes, Mrs. Brimhall," I say, and put my head down.

I hear her click off, pull out the photo, and stuff Polly into her padded pocket. By the time I look at the picture, it's finished developing.

Does it look cool because I'm sideways, with my head on the desk, or will it still look cool when I look at it the right way? I'm pretty sure it'll look awesome no matter how it's viewed.

I smile and close my eyes, resting until the bell rings.

Chapter 4
Wednesday

Perfect Hands Don't Hold Pencils

Porter saves me a seat in science class. It's a lab.

"How many kids did you have to fight off to keep my seat?" I ask. He gives me a high five as I sit on a stool next to him and sling my backpack onto the floor.

"Just three," he says, as he rubs his scratched glasses on his Star Wars T-shirt. "I got here a few seconds before you, so most everyone was sitting already."

"Glad you found a table away from Mr. Bine's stinky experiment." I point to the open office door on the other side of the room. "Let's set a record today. I've got math homework to finish."

"Roger that," Porter says. He folds a paper into smaller and smaller pieces but stops when Mr. Bines stands up front.

Mr. Bines is older than Einstein and his hair looks the same, except it's reddish grey.

"Class," he says, croaking it out in two syllables. "Today's assignment will be. . . ."

The door squeaks open, tickling my ears, and everyone turns to see who's coming in.

Perfectly manicured hands hand a green paper to Mr. Bines. The rest of her perfectly perfectness connected to the hands stands at the front of the room like a princess waiting for us to bow.

"Cherie Bodecker," he says, reading the note. "Welcome to third period General Science."

"It's pronounced Cher-EEE," say the perfectly pouting lips.

Blech!

"Yes, well, please go take the empty seat by Porter. He'll help you catch up."

Double blech!

Mr. Bines turns. "Porter, please stand so Ms. Bodecker knows where. . . ."

"I know Porter, Mr. Bines." And the perfectly perfect hair swishes our way.

"There goes our record," Porter whispers to me out of the corner of his mouth.

"There goes my math homework," I say, picturing another big, fat zero.

What is Dad going to say? How can I keep this from him? I press on my stomach to try and get rid of the knot inside.

Cherie gives the smelly garbage look she always uses on me and sits on the other side of the lab table. She even sits perfectly—a graceful slide onto the stool, hands folded gently in front of her.

19

"Alright class, for today's lab we'll continue studying the Classification System.

"You'll notice a box on each table. I want you to open the box and see how many ways you can categorize the 24 natural objects. Work as a group and make sure whoever takes notes has it legible."

Porter hands the notepad and pencil to Cherie. "Here, this'll be a good way for you to get your feet wet." He winks at me and I know he means it'll be a good way for me to get some math done. I pull my math book and homework out of my backpack, ready to get started.

"Um. I don't think so," Cherie says. "I'll watch."

Porter stares for a second. I roll my eyes at her and growl inside, dropping my math book into my backpack. Then I grab my science notebook and tear out a sheet of paper.

"We know you're not going to take notes, Porter. Bines will never be able to read it." I want to spit my words out and aim them at Cherie, but that will only make things worse, so I add a small smile.

Porter opens the box and pulls things out. Cherie sits and looks around, checks herself in her mirror, glances at her phone, and picks at her nails. Every once in a while she lifts something up, looks at it, and sets it down.

Porter and I almost read each other's minds. He takes the objects and starts to group them. I see how many groups he makes and put that many boxes on the paper. Then he sticks each object into a group. When I see his pattern, I help, if I'm caught up with writing. We work fast and have categorized things by color, size, hardness, and smoothness, and if it was ever alive or not.

Porter and I give each other a high five. Finally, something is good today.

Then Cherie speaks up.

"What about where you find them? And I don't mean the box." She pulls the items towards her and sorts them into five groups: ocean, beach, mountains, desert, and forest.

"Wait, wouldn't ocean and beach be the same?" Porter asks.

"Whatever," she says, picking at her nails again. How does she keep them so nice when she picks at them all the time?

"Here," I say. I smile, hoping that will help. "You write them down. I'm getting a hand cramp."

"Ew. No," she says, giving me the smelly garbage look before picking at her nails.

I sigh and go back to writing.

The bell rings and Porter puts the objects away, while I finish the last of the writing. Cherie ignores the work, lifts up her pretty little purse, and saunters away.

"What's her problem?" Porter asks.

"Me," I say, slinging my backpack over my shoulder. "She's hated me since third grade. See you later."

"Okay," Porter says. "Good luck with math."

"Math! Oh, crumb bum!" I yell, slapping my forehead. I run out of the room. Maybe I can get more done at lunch.

Chapter 5

Wednesday

Ms. Carter's Ten—Well, Four—Commandments

I scoot into math class as the late bell rings. Ms. Carter has her back to me, talking on the intercom with the office. Slipping into a seat a few seconds after the bell, I cross my fingers she doesn't turn around.

The boy next to me smells like he didn't shower after gym. I move my desk over as much as possible without looking obvious. I don't want Ms. Carter staring at me when she says her personal mantra on punctuality. Thinking of her stare makes me shiver.

"Class, I'm glad to see you all in your seats. Punctuality will get you somewhere in life. Punctuality, and completing your assignments on time. Please pass your homework to the front and the right. Then turn to page 68," Ms. Carter says, whining through her nose like she has a permanent cold. *She really ought to see a doctor about that*, I think, as I put my name on my pink pen scribbled homework page. At least I can turn in something.

"Class, page 68 please. . . ."

Ms. Carter's voice fades into muffled background noise, like construction going on down the street. I hear someone clear his throat behind me. Maybe he has a tickle and needs a cough drop. Someone clicks down the hall in high heels. It sounds like Mrs. Brimhall. A breeze comes through the open window, making the poster 'Love math, it loves you,' flap and snap. I love math, just not Ms. Carter. And Ms. Carter doesn't love us. She thinks she's a math god, bringing us enlightenment and giving us all sorts of rules to live by.

I think up rules she would have if she had the chance to give out her own commandments.

Ms. Carter's Ten Commandments
1) Thou shalt have no other classes before me.
2) Thou shalt bow down to me in all that I say.
3) Thou shalt be in thine seat with thine butt in thine chair before the bell ringeth.
4) Thou shalt use only an #2 pencil.

"Ms. Tanner, how would you solve that one?"

I look up. Everyone stares at me. Marsha Hickock gives me a supportive smile. Ms. Carter peers over her glasses.

Oh, crumb bum.

This must not be the first time she's called my name. She might give a second chance without writing a name on the board, but not a third. My body shivers again.

Thinking fast I come up with an excuse.

"Uh, I'm sorry Ms. Carter. I don't have my contacts today. Give me a second." While I talk, I scan the board, my book (luckily opened to the right page), and the clock (to judge if we might be farther along than I think). I figure it has to be problem number eleven. Since seven and nine were on the board, it was a pretty easy guess.

Bam! Nailed it.

"Very good, Ms. Tanner. I must have been mistaken, I thought you were not paying attention." She smiles, looking as though the cracks in her lips will drop little crumbles on her desk.

Whew. I try to listen harder. It works long enough for me to figure out the next concept. It's an easy one.

Tonight, I'll do my homework (with a #2 pencil, of course) right after dinner, put it straight in my folder in my backpack, and put my backpack by the door to my room. I picture the whole scene; sitting on my bed, with classical music turned down low, my lap board on my lap, my math book and paper on my lap board, my pencil in my hand, my brain thinking wonderful math thoughts. . . .

"Before you leave make sure you take a flier about Mathletes. I expect most of you will be interested. There will be more information on this and other clubs at tomorrow's assembly," Ms. Carter says, waving us out of the room.

My heart jumps. Mathletes sounds like a blast. Except that Ms. Carter is in charge. Maybe if Porter joins, too, it might be fun.

There's a low murmur as students pack up their things.

"Remember class, tomorrow there is an assembly during this period, so you will have an extra day for homework," Ms. Carter whines over the bell.

Great, I won't have to worry about homework tonight. I put my books away and dash towards the classroom door.

Hurrying to get to my locker before gym, the last class of the day, I scoot around Marsha, startling her.

CRASH!

Her books and papers fly everywhere.

"Good going, Mousy Marsha," says Tina, Cherie's friend.

Marsha blushes.

"Cut it out, Tina," I say, as I scoop up a handful of papers. They feel smooth as they slip across each other in my hands.

Marsha organizes her mess. "Thanks," she says in a breathy whisper, very mouse-like, pushing some stray hairs behind her ear.

She doesn't look quite so mousy when she smiles.

"Hey, my fault for scaring the bejeebies out of you," I say, shrugging. I run down the hall. "See ya later," I yell.

I hope someone being nice to her makes up for that brainless cheerleader comment. Some people. Ugh.

Chapter 6
Wednesday Afternoon

Pink Icing and Pretty Ponies

After school, I stuff some old math papers from my locker into the bottom of my backpack. The garbage truck comes in the morning and I want to dump them when I take the can to the street. I also grab my new photos and wrap a paper around them, then slide them in a book inside my backpack. I can show them to Porter on the bus ride home.

But what if he doesn't see what I see? What if the pictures aren't cool? I've only taken pictures for a few weeks, since I got the camera on my thirteenth birthday. Maybe I don't know what I'm doing and they look stupid.

I shake my head, slam my locker door, and run to the bus.

Porter talks about Mathletes on the bus. He jabbers like a parrot. I wonder if Ms. Carter will let me join the club. I wonder if I want to join the club. My mind jabbers faster than Porter can talk.

As Cherie and Tina pass my seat for their stop, Tina drops a crunched-up paper in my lap. It reads:

Never ask Cherie to write. Do it yourself, jerk.

Porter looks over my shoulder. "What's that about?"

"Just Cherie being lazy," I say. I stuff the paper in my backpack. "I'm not doing her work for her."

Walking in the door at home, I jump over Mason's roller blades, sidestep Jada and her baby walker, and run from Sarah's gluey pink fingers before she grabs my jeans. A wonderful smell comes from the kitchen.

"Mom, I'm home," I yell.

"In the kitchen," she calls back. "I'm making angel food cake with strawberry whipped cream frosting."

"Yum," I say, coming to the counter. I stick my finger in the bowl with the frosting and let its sticky sweetness coat my tongue. The yumminess melts away some of the icky thoughts about Cherie and school.

I sprint upstairs to put my backpack away while the thought is in my head.

My plan is to come back down for a big spoon filled with peanut butter. That will hit the empty spot in my stomach until dinner. I throw my backpack into the corner of my room and hop down the stairs.

"Bly, why don't you show me your schoolwork? Have you got any papers for me to see or sign?" Mom says as I enter the kitchen.

The icing in my stomach churns. What can I tell Mom? *Think, Bly, think.* I try to look innocent.

Sarah runs into the room. "Mason said I was ugly," Sarah says, as she cries onto Mom's leg, her straggly, blond hair whipping around as her head turns.

Mom picks her up, flips her around, and takes her to the sink.

Mason comes in, his shorts falling off his skinny rear end. "No I didn't, Sarah. I said your shirt was ugly."

"It is not. It has pretty ponies on it," Sarah says.

"Yeah, but the pink icing by their mouths makes them look like they're throwing up."

"Horses can't throw up. Don't you even know that?" Sarah says.

This is my chance to get out of Mom's sight. I head out of the kitchen.

"That's enough you two. Bly, get back here."

Caught.

"I don't remember why I called you, but while you're here, I'm doing a load of darks soon. Bring your dirties down, and make sure you put those jeans in the basket. And the pants with the cherry stain. She pauses and studies my jeans. "Is that ink on there?" Not waiting for an answer, she wrestles with Sarah again.

"Sarah, go change your shirt so I can wash this before the stain sets. Mason, put away your roller blades. You left them near the front door. And push Jada back in here. I think she's worked her way to the front door."

I back out of the room.

"Bly," she stops to help pull Sarah's shirt over her head.

I am so dead. She remembered. The only papers I've got have big red zeros on them.

My body feels heavy like every cell suddenly weighs

28

ten pounds. If I show her, she'll know I'm not her smart girl anymore. Then she'll tell Dad, and I won't be his little professor. I'll be his flunky. He'll hate me.

I have to get my grades up without them knowing. It's still September. My grades can't be terminal yet.

"Um, yes?"

"How's school going?"

Distract her. That might work.

"Um. . . fine," I say, the icing still tossing in my stomach. "We have an assembly tomorrow about the school clubs. There's a math club I might want to join."

"Oh, let's make sure to tell Dad about that. He used to be in Mathletes."

"Yeah, that's it," I say, starting up the stairs. "That sounds awesome." I'm good at math and fast. Competing could be a blast. I back up the stairs, hoping to get away without more questions.

When I'm in my room, I jump on the bed and sigh. Maybe I'm failing math, but failing has gotta be Carter's fault, with all her rules. Somehow I'll have to figure out how to pass even with all the rules.

I just need to try harder.

I jump back out of bed and skip over to my backpack. I pull my book out and gently pick up today's pictures. I open my nightstand and hide them under my too-small nightgown with all the other pictures I've taken.

"Now you're safe," I say. "Cherie can't get to you anymore."

29

Chapter 7

Things About My Dad

1. His closet has his clothes in rainbow color order, with matching hangers.

2. He color coordinates our family calendar. I'm pink.

3. He loves meatloaf, but doesn't like it when the piece breaks before it gets to his plate (He'll eat it anyway, he isn't crazy).

4. He likes making and following rules.

5. He's a very smart professor (I've heard him called brilliant).

6. He thinks I'm smarter than he is (He must not be brilliant).

Chapter 8
Thursday Morning

My Family and the Rain Give Me the Frizzies

Breakfast," Mom yells.

I'm almost ready. My hair is a mess because of the rain, so I pull it back in a ponytail. When I glance in the mirror the rest of my hair is frizzing around my face. I stick my tongue out at myself and skip down to the kitchen.

Dad is at the table, finishing a bowl of corn flakes. "Hey, Professor. What are you doing downstairs and dressed before we've called you five times?" he asks. He picks up his bowl and takes it to the sink, kissing the top of my head as he passes.

"Pure luck," I say, as I reach across the table for the cereal. My insides cringe hearing myself called 'professor,' but I paste on my fake smile anyway.

"Mom said you get to find out about clubs today. You know I was the captain of our Mathletes team, don't you?"

"She didn't tell me you were captain. That sounds cool."

"She didn't tell you I was captain?" Dad takes the dishtowel in his hand and gives Mom a playful swat. She giggles.

"To be fair, the kids were a bit. . . busy when we were talking about it." She gives Dad a kiss and turns to me. "Your dad helped the team make it to State. And then they got to travel to. . . where was it, sweetie?"

"Las Vegas for regionals." Dad and Mom look at each other as if no one else is in the room. It makes me sigh every time they do that.

Jada bangs on her high chair with her spoon. The sound bangs into my ears, making it hard to think about anything else.

"Could you put another handful of cereal in front of her, Bly?" Mom asks. The banging stops as soon as I drop some flakes in front of her. Mom pulls Mason out from under the sink. "No screwdrivers without Daddy helping." She takes a large screwdriver with a red handle from Mason's hand.

"But I was fixing the dishwasher," he says.

"The dishwasher is working fine, Son," Dad says. "Go get your backpack. We'll talk about what we can fix together on the drive to school."

"Dad's team would have won regionals, except your dad got sick," Mom says.

"Bad case of the stomach flu. Couldn't leave the hotel room." Dad grabs a bagged lunch from the counter.

"And his specialty, binomials, was the last question."

They both laugh, but I can tell Dad's laugh is kind of forced, like it still hurt when he thinks about it.

"We'll see if you can break the Tanner curse. No stomach

flu allowed." He winks at me.

Sarah comes into the kitchen as I add homemade rhubarb jam to my toast. She's dressed only in a pair of pink underwear, her pale belly covered in goose bumps. "I can't find my pretty pony shirt." As she speaks, she jumps up and down in front of Mom so close, it looks as though Mom will tumble right over her.

"It's in the washer, love. You'll have to choose something else." Mom picks Sarah up under the armpits, gives her a raspberry on the tummy, and puts her back down, facing the other direction. "I think your Super Princess shirt is clean. Go!" She gives Sarah a light pat on the bum and turns to the counter to cut some banana for Jada.

Dad puts his lunch in his briefcase. "We'll talk more about it later." He kisses Mom again and heads to the garage with Mason.

I hear the bus coming as I set my dishes in the sink and wash the stickiness off my fingers. The bus makes a loud hum along with a grinding noise and the dog next-door barks every morning before the bus makes it around the corner. Being one of the first stops, it's never crowded when it gets to my house, but when the weather is nice and the windows are down, I can hear the kids inside. Not today. It's dripping and dreary.

I run upstairs for my backpack and almost trip over Sarah. "Sorry, Sarah."

"That's okay. You missed," she says.

I bounce down the stairs and out the door. Mom is holding up the bus again. I blush, seeing her standing there in her red, fluffy bathrobe. She hands me my rain jacket.

"Thanks, Mom, I guess. Maybe next time you can get dressed first?" I don't stop for the kiss she probably wants.

"Maybe next time you can be on time?" She shuffles up the stairs as I bounce down.

Chapter 9
Thursday

Poor Polly Isn't In Her Pocket

I see Marsha as we file into the gym for the assembly. The noise hits me like a firecracker and I cover my ears.

"Do you want to sit with me?" I shout.

Marsha smiles and nods. Then she says something.

"What?" I ask, seeing her lips move.

She points to her ears and I drop one hand from mine to listen.

"The noise isn't so bad," she says. "Is that guy waving at you?"

"Come on, that's Porter. Let's sit by him." I grab her arm and pull her across the gym floor to the bleachers. Porter is two rows up and moves over to make room.

"Look," he says. "There's got to be at least thirty different clubs. How are we going to decide which one to join?"

"You can join more than one," Marsha says, her head barely peeking up at Porter, her face bright red. "At least when my sister was going here you could."

"Oh, yeah," I say. "Marsha, this is Porter. Porter, this is Marsha."

"I think you're in my English class," Porter says.

Marsha smiles and colors again.

The Principal, Mr. Stormsby, walks to the microphone. His big stomach jiggles as he plods forward. The microphone gives a big whistle and I cover my ears again until it stops. Most of the kids keep talking until Mr. Kamai, the vice principal with no fat to jiggle, only giant muscles, comes forward and crosses his arms, giving the crowd his don't-mess-with-me look. Everyone settles down and Mr. Stormsby begins his speech.

"You may ask, my dear young friends, why we consider participation in clubs to be integral to success here at Rockport Junior High. Let me read you a quote from. . . ."

I yawn and pull Polly out of her pocket. We aren't supposed to take pictures in classes or assemblies, but my fingers itch to touch my camera. I'm not hurting anything. No one will notice.

The bleachers have weird lighting and angles. I look behind Marsha and see a deep gap between her navy shirt and the bench. It looks like a bottomless pit. I twist funny, aim Polly, and shoot. Polly whines out the picture and I pull it off, waving the picture around like a flag down at my side. Polly goes back to her safe place.

"What are you doing?" Marsha whispers. "Is that a camera?"

Click, click, click.

A familiar pencil pull swings in my face. Mrs. Brimhall

holds out her hand.

My stomach drops faster than Polly's shutter speed and I swallow so I don't throw up.

"Do I have to?" I ask.

"I'm afraid so, Blythe Tanner. I expected more of you."

I gently place the picture in her outstretched hand, developing side up. It isn't finished, but it looks like it'll turn out too dark anyway.

"The camera, please."

"Oh, no. Please don't take my camera. I'll leave it in my backpack, I promise."

"You know the rules, Ms. Tanner. You may have it back after school."

I reverently pull Polly out from her safe place and hand her to Mrs. Brimhall. "Please be careful with her," I say as Mrs. Brimhall clicks away.

Marsha pats me on the back. I give her a sort of smile, knowing she's being kind, even though it isn't much help.

I try to listen to Mr. Stormsby, though I can barely keep my body still. I want to chase after Mrs. Brimhall and beg her to give Polly back.

"And so, no running as you wind your way around the tables. When you've finished your tour, please take all of your papers and file through to the other side of the gym where the folk dance club will entertain you until the bell rings. Thank you, Rockport students, for your fine behavior today."

Mr. Stormsby backs away from the mike and the noise explodes—worse than when we came in. I sit for a minute, my hands on my ears until most everyone is off the bleachers. It isn't just the noise, but my chest is still pounding and my eyes are full, threatening to spill over.

Porter comes over and grabs my arm, pulls my hand off my ear, and me off my seat.

"Wait, I need my backpack." I turn and see Cherie hobbling down the bleachers in heels. Some boy from ninth grade comes over and takes her hand. She gives him a big smile as he helps her down the rest of the steps.

"Come on, Bly," Porter says. "I want time to see every table."

"I'm hoping they have a science club," Marsha says.

Porter points. "Science club over that way."

"Mind if we split up?" Porter asks.

"No problem," I say and head to the tables. Marsha makes a beeline towards the science club.

I stand still and watch the mass of kids swarming the tables, like aquarium fish being fed. I square my shoulders and dive in.

There's a sea of kids in front of me as I work my way forward, trying not to step on anyone's feet. The first booth I get to is Mathletes. Some big guy with a green t-shirt in front of me moves away and I see Ms. Carter sitting behind the table. She nods at some students and frowns at others.

I gulp.

She sees me and frowns.

"Pink marker, Ms. Tanner? Scrap paper? You know the rules."

My face gets hot and I peek around to see who else hears her. And who might hear me. No one's looking. I take a deep breath. "But I'd done it at home. Really. I just forgot to bring it."

"You have used that excuse already. I did not count it then and I will not count it now."

I take a deep breath and spit out another excuse. "I had to go to a funeral." It was true, but my legs start shaking. If she asks me any questions, what will I say?

"Oh! I'm sorry to hear that, Ms. Tanner. Was it someone close?" Ms. Carter looks concerned. I've never seen her look concerned.

Before I can stop myself I blurt something out. "My brother. . . well, my stepbrother."

Argh! Why did I say that?

Ms. Carter's mouth bobs open and shut but no words come out.

I have to get away from here before I say something else stupid. I grab a flyer and run. . . straight into Cherie. Her heels fly up, almost hitting me in the chin and she lands back in the arms of the guy who'd helped her down the bleachers. He smiles like a hero, with his prize in his arms, while Cherie glares at me. I thought the garbage look was bad; this look is more like a death laser.

"Sorry," I say, before scooching myself away.

Out of the corner of my eye, I see a few letters of a sign 'Pho. . . y.' Maybe, just maybe it's what I'm looking for. Getting closer, I see it. Photography.

There's a photography club!

At the table sits a hairy guy I don't know and my geography teacher—Mr. Scott. My voice shakes as I ask the big question. "Do you have to know what you're doing to be in this club? Is there, like, a test or something?"

"No test, Bly. Just a love of photography. We'll learn and practice a number of skills."

"Cool," I say. I sign my name, grab a flyer, and run off.

I don't think to ask what day either club meets.

Chapter 10
Thursday

Why Can't Life Be As Simple As PBJ?

I wander through the clubs until the bell rings for late lunch. Since everyone has late lunch, I feel like I'm in some kind of shuffle game, being pushed forward, backward, and sideways, until I work my way to a half-empty table. My stomach twists and it isn't hunger.

Why did I say that to Ms. Carter? What if she asks me questions about my stepbrother, the lizard?

Well, Ms. Carter. His name was Lester. How did he die? My mother said he just got old. We only had him a few years, but he could have been old when we first got him.

Nope. Maybe I could pretend I've got some disease and can't talk anymore.

What I really need to do is start planning my own funeral.

Until then, the clubs. Mathletes sounds okay, but photography club sounds amazing. I guess I can be in both, but do I even want to be around Ms. Carter that much? The more I think about it, the worse it sounds.

I hope Marsha can find me in this swarm of kids. I'd asked her to sit with me. I lay both the math flyer and the photography flyer in front of me to read while I eat. May as well plan my funeral with a full stomach. As I pull my sandwich out of the bag, I hear a voice behind me.

"Can I sit down?" Cherie takes the seat next to me. Her hair is back behind a pink and brown headband that matches the rest of her outfit. Her nails look like she's painted them that morning.

I pull my lip-gloss out of my pocket and cover my lips, even though I'll eat it off with the first bite of sandwich. It feels like a layer of protection against her meanness. "I guess that's fine," I say, looking into her eyes and ignoring the sparklers going off in my stomach. "As long as you don't plan on being rude." I force myself not to blink.

She blinks. "Whatever."

I turn my head and take a bite of my sandwich. Plain old peanut butter and jelly. Smooth. And grape. On wheat. About as honest a sandwich as you can get. I swallow and feel a lump inch its way down. "So, what do you want?" I ask, looking her in the eye again.

"Yeah, well," she says, not touching her food. She looks around as if the room is full of spies. "I saw how you and Porter worked so well together in science." She pauses and looks around again.

"Yeah?"

"Cheerleading has got me tied up, like 5 days a week,

42

and this is my weekend with my dad. He's got a trip to the city planned for us."

"Yeah?"

"Well, so, I thought you could do that science report for me." She brushes her hair back with her hand and gives me a big eye look.

"What?" The peanut butter gets stuck in my throat. I gag and grab my milk, sipping down most of it.

Cherie talks again before I can say more. "I'll do something for you. Maybe. . . sign some kind of permission slip or progress report you don't want your parents to see? I'm really good at scrawling signatures. Or, maybe I could pay you. Dad gives me a big allowance."

I stare at her. Miss Perfect cheats. "Um, I don't think so. Sorry."

She goes into a stare. I think maybe she's in shock that someone said no to her. I follow her eyes and see Marsha coming to our table. "I'll catch you later. Don't say anything."

Cherie stands, takes her tray in her hand with her freshly polished fingernails, and moves from the table. I watch her hair swish back and forth until she gets to her regular seat. She sits next to Tina and the two of them whisper, heads together like the football team in a huddle.

"Thanks for asking me to sit with you." Marsha looks at me with her mousy smile. I see a tinge of hope in her eyes, mixed with a tinge of fear.

If I say 'boo,' she'll be gone before the 'oo' is.

"Sure," I say, and try to give a gentle smile. It's like

putting out your hand to a scared animal, slow and easy. It seems like ages since I've had that warm, giving feeling. *Am I being selfish, worrying about my own problems so much?* "Grab a seat."

Marsha sits and fiddles with her milk spout. It gives her a hard time, fighting for its life. She finally wins. Sort of. It opens with a rip down the side. "I'm gonna go get a straw," she says.

When she leaves, I look back at Cherie's table. No more whispering. They're having a typical day at the popular table. A football player visits with his foot on a chair, his elbow on his knee, waving his arms around, and talking about something that gets them laughing.

I won't think about what Cherie asked me. The peanut butter should stick to my ribs, not in my throat.

Marsha comes back with her straw. She sits quietly as she eats. It's fine because it gives me time to think about Cherie. I never thought she was a cheater.

Looking back at Cherie's table, I catch her eye. She gives me a stare that says, 'don't tell.' My stomach spins along with my head. No one has ever asked me to help them cheat.

But getting a fake signature on a progress report is more tempting than I want to admit.

"Has anyone ever asked you to do something you don't want to do?" I ask, breaking our silence.

Marsha turns a little pink before she answers. It's kind of splotchy, getting lighter as it goes higher up her face "I guess," she says. "Probably."

"What did you do?"

"I don't know. I can't think of anything right now," she says, taking a sip of her milk. "But Grandma always says, 'you can't control what other people do. Only what you do.'"

I think about that for a moment. It makes some sense. I glance at Cherie, careful that it isn't obvious. Right then someone passes by and throws a paper over his shoulder. I catch it before it gets to the floor.

It's a flyer for Mathletes.

Mathletes
REMEMBER!!!
You must see Ms. Carter (room A4) by September 18th at 3:00 pm to join the fun
Question: If it is now September 15th, 11:00 am, how many more hours do you have before it is too late?? Think fast!!

Easy—76. If only my math grade were that high.

Chapter 11
Thursday

Polly Want A Screwdriver?

After school, I get my picture and camera back from Mrs. Brimhall.

"This is an interesting picture, Blythe, but please pay attention when you are supposed to pay attention."

I nod and run off, hoping to make it to the bus before it leaves. I also stop by Mr. Scott's room because I can't find my flyer for the photography club.

Mr. Scott says, "I figured you'd come for a flyer again, Bly. First one went. . . ?"

"Um. . . into the Carpathian Mountains?"

Mr. Scott laughs. "Make sure you've got that homework tomorrow."

"I will," I shout, as I scoot out the door, though I can't remember what homework he's talking about.

Not wanting to miss my bus, I hurry past my locker and out the side door without stopping for my backpack or anything, paper and picture in one hand, camera in the other.

Asteroid is closing the door and pulling forward.

"Wait, wait," I call, waving my arms in the air. The bus jerks to a stop, the door opens, and I hop on, half out of breath.

"Thanks, Ast. . . um, thanks for stopping," I say. I feel my face itching. It flushes so fast. As far as I know, he has no idea everyone calls him Asteroid.

"Hey, you can call me Asteroid if I can call you Fly Girl." Asteroid swings the door closed.

"Fly Girl?" I ask as I head down the aisle.

"Like I said the other day, you're always on the fly." He turns the music up and starts the bus.

"Sit down, Fly Girl," he says, making a grinding sound with the bus as he turns the wheel.

The bus moves right before I sit, and I fly into Cherie's lap.

Cherie pushes me off and speaks to her seat neighbor. "Fly Girl, because she's as annoying as a fly."

The flush that began to fade from my cheeks flares back up and I slide in next to Porter.

"Don't worry about her," Porter says. "She has to find something to complain about or she feels useless."

I nod and look down at the floor on the aisle. Something catches my eye, but I can't quite figure out what it is. I pick Polly up off my lap and look through the viewfinder. It doesn't look right. I need to be closer.

Asteroid seems to be paying attention to driving and no one else seems to be looking, so I step out into the aisle and bend over. Still not close enough. I get down onto my knees

47

and my elbows, the camera up to my eye. The floor smells like dust and grease. I bend forward, and it's looking better and better.

I think it's a couple of scratches with scuff marks around them. I'm not sure. I just know that through the viewfinder it looks amazing. Like some kind of alien design in the middle of a desert, maybe. I press the button and. . . Click. No whirring sound comes.

The bus stops and kids trample all over me as they head for the door. Cherie's shoe comes into focus and I pull back, protecting Polly next to my chest, afraid she might kick my camera. Looking up at her, I see her roll her eyes before she moves up the aisle and out the door.

Everyone who's leaving is out of the bus and I'm sitting on the floor. My chin didn't hit the ground this time, but I'm sure to have bruises all over my legs.

"Hey, Fly Girl," says Asteroid, "back in your seat."

I pull myself up and plop down next to Porter, my camera still held protectively against my chest, no picture whirring out to develop in front of me. I lean back against the seat and close my eyes tight to keep the tears in.

"I think my camera is broken."

Chapter 12
Thursday Afternoon

Oh Where, Oh Where Has My Manual Gone?

I walk in the door with Polly and the new picture from the assembly. I have to hide Polly, who my parents don't allow at school, so I stay quiet and scoot upstairs to my room, then come down to the kitchen, where Sarah and Mason are giving Mom a concert with Sarah's play instruments. They are whisper singing and playing, which means Jada is asleep.

"Oh, hey Bly. I didn't hear you come in." Mom puts away the cup in her hand and comes over for a hug. "I've got a tray of vegetables cut up and some dip. Sit down and enjoy the concert."

"Can I take some to my room? I've got something to work on."

"Oh. Yeah. Sure. Let me grab you a plate."

"You should stay and listen," Sarah says, breaking from her singing to look at me.

"Yeah," says Mason. "We've been practicing all afternoon. We're really good."

I take a deep breath. Sarah gives me her doe eyes.

"Okay. I'll stay for a minute." I sit at the table, crunching carrots with Mom, and listen to the budding musicians.

After a few songs they stand and bow and we give our whisper cheers and pretend claps.

"I gotta go potty," Sarah says, and runs off, holding herself.

Mason takes the toy tambourine and begins to study it. If Sarah doesn't hurry back, he'll have it in a dozen pieces.

"So, how was school?" Mom asks.

I choke a bit on my carrot and cough. It gives me a minute to think how I can answer.

"We had our club assembly today."

"Oh, wonderful! Dad's been so excited to talk to you about Mathletes. He told me more stories about his experiences last night after you went to bed. Did you know Mathletes was a major factor in his getting a scholarship to the University of Illinois?"

"No, I didn't. Cool."

"Did they give you a flyer or something we can look at?" Mom stands, taking the vegetable tray. "Mason, those toys belong to Sarah. You'll need her permission to take them apart."

Mason sighs and puts down the tambourine.

"Maybe. . . I'm not sure. I'll look upstairs."

"Alright, hun. Bring what you have down for dinner. We'll talk about it then."

I run upstairs, grab Polly from my dresser and sit on the

bed, eager to figure out what's wrong with her.

"The manual. Where's the manual?"

I pull out drawers and hunt through each one, even my underwear drawer. No luck. A few things drop on the floor, but I'll worry about that later. I open my closet. A tennis racket and sweatshirt fall out right away but nothing in the closet looks like the instructions, printed in four different languages. I dig into any area in my room that looks like it can hold Polly's care manual.

Fifteen minutes later, I give up, sit on the floor with Polly in my hand, and sigh. I decide to try and take another picture. Click. . . nothing.

"The internet!" I shout, running out of my room with Polly in my hand. "Mom, what's today's password?" I yell down the stairs, hoping Mom is in the kitchen so she can hear me.

"Shhh! PollyWantACracker," she whispers loudly. "Each word capitalized. Twenty minutes, I'm setting the timer."

"Thanks. That should be enough," I loud whisper back.

Polly is in the password. It's a good sign.

It takes two minutes to find the online manual. I go straight to 'troubleshooting."

It takes thirty seconds to find out what's wrong.

I'm out of film.

Price—$32 for 24 pictures.

It might as well be $3200.

Chapter 13
Thursday Evening

Failure Level—100

"Pass the meatloaf, please," Dad says, ready for seconds.

"Can I have an advance on my allowance?" I ask.

"Why?" Dad asks, helping himself to meatloaf. It comes out in one piece. *Good juju?*

"I need more film for my camera." The meatloaf's good, but I'm worried about figuring out how to pay for film, not filling my stomach.

"How much?" Mom asks.

"It costs $32 a roll. I have $3.50," I say. It's hopeless. I know they won't advance me three weeks' worth. I take a bite of meatloaf but it tastes like the unsolved math problems I won't be able to do tonight without my book. I turn my head and spit the meatloaf into my napkin.

"You've had that camera for a while now. You haven't added new film to your budget?" Dad takes a swig of his milk.

Jada's tray is empty and she bangs on it. My ears flinch inside.

"I think Jada likes your meat loaf as much as I do," Dad says, winking at Mom.

"I didn't think about it," I say. I give what I hope is a 'forgive me' smile.

"Then, I suppose we'll think about it. I'll give you an answer later." Dad wipes his mouth with his napkin. "Now, let's talk about Mathletes."

"There were a lot of cool clubs, including. . . ."

Dad gives me the 'don't interrupt' look. "I looked it up online and saw that they meet on Tuesday afternoons." He glanced at the color-coded calendar on the kitchen wall. "That should work fine for you."

I nod.

"But I also saw that they have an entrance exam. Which makes sense, because you don't want to have anyone slow down the group."

I nod again.

"That shouldn't be a problem for you, based on what I saw from last year's test scores, but I think we should spend some time studying together to make sure you're up to speed."

Another nod from me. "Can I also. . . ."

"Wait a minute, Bly. Let me finish. The online information also said you need to have a "C" average in order to participate. I assume that isn't a problem? You remember that Tanners are expected to get A's?" He looks back and forth between Mom and me. "Have you been getting progress reports yet?"

My heart sinks so far, I don't know if I'll ever get it back where it belongs.

Dad loves me for being smart. He loves Mason for his curiosity, Sarah for her enthusiasm, Jada, well, cause she's a baby. But me? It's for my brains.

What if he knows I'm not smart? Will he still love me? I know he sort of will because he has to—he's my dad. But will he really love me? Will he still think I'm special?

I don't want to find out. There must be a way to keep my parents in the dark until I can bring my grades up. I have to find a way.

Oh, but that picture. I lift my hands and look through the rectangle of my fingers. The way the shadow of my fork stretches out across the tablecloth and meets with the shadow of my glass looks like some cool science project.

I have to get money for more film.

"I haven't seen any progress reports yet," Mom says. "Bly?"

I slip my hands under the table. "Um, I can ask about them tomorrow," I say. That isn't quite a lie. Still, the meatloaf left on my plate now looks gross—all greasy and slimy.

As icky as I feel over trying to fool my parents, something still nags at me. I swallow hard and open my mouth. "Is it okay for me to join more than one club? Cause I really want to join the photography club."

If I can join photography club, everything else will be okay. It won't matter quite so much if Dad never thinks of me as his little professor. It won't matter if I'm not the best student in the world. I don't even think Cherie's dirty looks will bug me anymore.

"I don't see a problem with that," Mom says. "I think you should be able to handle a second club."

Before I can react, Dad chimes in. "I studied the schedule. Photography club conflicts with Mathletes. Find something else. We'll start practicing after I make a phone call."

With that, Dad thanks Mom for dinner and excuses himself.

Chapter 14
Friday

If I Whisper, Is It Real?

Thirty dollars and I'll help you, not do it for you." My whisper is so soft, I'm not sure Cherie hears me.

She stops and faces me. "Help me?"

"Yeah. That way it doesn't feel like. . . cheating." The last word I only mouth. I glance around. Here we are in the middle of a crowded hall and I'm doing something as close to cheating as I've ever done. But hours of thought made me realize this is the only solution. I have to get money for more film. With my $3.50, and Mom and Dad's advance of $5.00, I need close to $30.00 more. With shipping and tax, I still might not have enough.

"I told you I'll be in Chicago this weekend. I don't have time." Cherie walks off.

"I've got it all worked out," I shout.

She stops and I catch up to her.

"We can chat on the computer. I'll get it all typed up and you can turn it in."

"You do the writing. And, for $30, I better get a good grade." Cherie walks on ahead of me.

"You will. I promise," I answer to her back. If she hears me, she doesn't show it. She just keeps walking.

I stop for a minute to let her get ahead of me before we go into science class. Maybe I'm being overly cautious, but since we never walk together, we shouldn't start now.

And that's when I see it. Posted over the water fountain.

Photography Contest
Theme:
"Tell Us A Story In Six Pictures"
Six winners will attend the opening of the Chacaran Gallery in Chicago, featuring guest photographer,
Jennifer Gardoney.
See Mr. Scott for details.

"Jennifer Gardoney. In person!" I whisper.

Somehow I find my way into science class, because when I blink, I'm sitting next to Porter and Mr. Bines is speaking.

"We've been studying classification now for a week. I hope you saw from your lab how many choices there are when classifying things. Can you imagine the challenges in creating such a system for life on earth?"

All I can imagine is meeting Jennifer Gardoney and getting a chance to talk to her about her photographs. Maybe even showing her one of mine.

Resting my head on my hand, my elbow on the lab table, I

let my mind go. It can't focus on Mr. Bines anyway.

"So nice to meet you, Ms. Tanner." Jennifer smiles with sparkling eyes.

"Oh, please, call me Bly."

"Of course. And you call me Jennifer."

"You're my favorite photographer. I love how your pictures make me think."

"Well, thank you. And let me see what you have there?"

"Oh, it's nothing. Just a picture I took with my Polaroid."

"Bly, this is magnificent. It reminds me of sand dunes at sunset. But, somehow, I don't think that's what it is."

"Bly, let's go."

"What?"

"Come on, class is over." Porter stands before me, giving me a shake on the shoulder.

I stand too, gather my things, and walk out the door, still thinking about meeting my favorite photographer.

Chapter 15
Friday

Someone Suspects

*S*he was being chased by at least a dozen horses. Did she *dare glance behind her to see how close they were getting? No, she must keep going. She pushed her steed harder, lowering her head onto his neck, and giving him a little more rein. He responded by pouring his heart out in his pace and the sound of the hoofs behind her began to fade slowly. Oh, so slowly. She wanted to close her eyes and pretend she was far away. Anywhere but in the forest. How far must it be to Bayern?*

"Bly, please come up and show us the Carpathian Mountains."

I shake my head and blink. Class. Oh. Geography. Oh.

"Umm, yeah, Just a second." I bend down to tie my shoe to give me time to clear my head. I walk to the map of Europe up front. "Which mountains did you say?" I figure with the shoe-tying I can have the excuse of forgetting what he said, instead of admitting I was somewhere in *Goose Girl* land.

"Carpathian," Mr. Scott says, giving me a smile. He saunters across the front of the classroom, smacking the pointer in one hand against the palm of the other. He's decent looking for an old guy; he must be at least thirty, with broad shoulders and blondish hair. And he never, ever yells. Oh, to have all teachers like Mr. Scott, instead of Ms. Carter.

"They go in a moon shape, right here." I point to the spot on the map, smile back at Mr. Scott, and walk to my seat.

"Very good, Bly, thank you. Chester, point out the Pyrenees."

Chester scratches his sandy blond curls with his pencil. "That's a trick question. Pyrenees is a kind of dog. My aunt has one." There's giggling from around the room. The kid behind me makes a sound like he is letting air out of a balloon little by little. Chester looks around. I don't think he's joking.

"You're right, Chester, it is a kind of dog. But it's also a mountain range. Look for it on page 102, and come show it to us on the big map. While he's looking that up, I'd like Ben to come and point out the Balkan Mountains.

As soon as class is over, I'll ask Mr. Scott about the contest, and more about photography club. Maybe he can change the day they meet so I can do both math and photography.

Dad isn't against photography club, he just doesn't want it to interfere with Mathletes. I'll put up with Ms. Carter if I can also go to photography club. And maybe with a few pointers, I'll have a chance to win the contest and meet my favorite photographer. And maybe she'll like my work and maybe she'll tell me how she became so famous and maybe. . . .

"I'll see you all tomorrow. Don't forget to write down

your homework assignment."

On the way out of class, Mr. Scott asks me to wait for a minute.

Great. He knows I'd been out of it.

I paste on a smile, even though I feel like slinking away.

"Bly," he says, crossing his arms over his chest. "You seem to have a knack for geography. Tell me where in the world you were today." He smiles like we're sharing a secret.

My face gets hot. "I don't know what you mean," I say, knowing he knows I'm lying.

Why do I do this lying thing? It always makes my stomach hurt.

"You don't?" he asks, lifting his eyebrows and cocking his head. "Well, young lady, if you ever decide you do know what I mean, you can come talk to me anytime." He looks at the clock over the door. "Now, you'd better get to your next period."

I run off as fast as I can. Halfway to math class, I remember that I haven't asked him about the contest or the club.

Then I remember that Ms. Carter thinks my stepbrother is dead.

Chapter 16
Friday

The Big Bad Math Teacher

I run down the hall, knowing I won't make it to class on time. Ms. Carter's room is at the far end of a different hall, with no shortcut.

Surrounded by ancient lockers, probably older than my parents, this part of the building was the first built. The corridors are thin, the lockers large, with lots of dents, and everything smells like paint thinner from the nearby art room. The math hall is clear of other kids by the time I get there; the only noise comes from my feet, the squeaky sneaker sound echoing off the lockers.

"Settle down," whines a familiar voice, as a door slams.

I skid to a stop in front of Ms. Carter's room. My sneakers give a final squeal. I can hear her muffled voice through the door and see her shadow through the thick glass. If I can time things so that her back is turned. . . .

The door gives a tiny creak as I open it enough to peek in. Ms. Carter is facing the board.

I swing the door open the rest of the way and dash to the empty seat by Marsha.

"Class, homework to the front and. . . Ms. Tanner? Thank you for gracing us with your presence." Ms. Carter writes my name in large letters for everyone to see. "After school today, Ms. Tanner. And I personally want to see your homework. Please bring it to me. Now."

I want to melt in my seat like lava spilling down a mountainside.

I wonder if the Carpathian Mountains have any volcanoes?

While everyone around me pulls out their work, I grab a blank paper to take to her desk, so no one else will know how stupid I am. So stupid I don't even remember to bring home my backpack so I can do homework.

Marsha gives me a smile of sympathy. That helps a little. But when you're drowning in an ocean of shame, taking away a bucketful doesn't do much.

"Your homework, Ms. Tanner," Ms. Carter says, holding out her hand.

"I, um. . . I don't have it," I say, bracing myself as if she's going to hit me.

But her words hit harder than her fist can. "Late, and no homework again. You will turn in tonight's homework before you leave my room this afternoon. And, I will be calling your parents. You may be mourning, but if you are not ready to fully participate in school, you should be at home."

I stare at her for a moment. She thinks my stepbrother has died and she still won't give me a break.

But she can't call my parents.

I've got to fix this without them. I can't let them know how stupid I am. And what if she asks about my dead stepbrother?

"No," I say, louder than I mean to.

I hear someone snicker on the front row.

"I was, um. . . I was late because Mr. Scott kept me after class. Please. Please don't call my parents. I'll stay and do my homework, just don't call my parents." I feel my eyes fill with tears. If I cry in class, I might as well put a bag over my head for the rest of the year. I bite my lip to distract my eyes. One silent tear falls down my cheek.

Ms. Carter clears her throat. "I will consider your excuse for tardiness. Back to your seat."

A whoosh of hope runs through me as I bounce to my seat. I do a quick tear wipe, disguised as scratching, and pull out my lip-gloss before I sit.

Marsha squeezes my arm and shows me her book. I open mine to the same page and pretend to concentrate on what the teacher is saying.

Why do I even want to be in Mathletes, with Ms. Carter leading the group? I love math, but I have enough of her with this class.

But how can I tell my dad and ruin his hopes for me?

I set my head on my hands and try to pay attention for the rest of class.

Chapter 17
Friday

Y-Intercept?

Mr. Scott verified the reason for your lateness, Ms. Tanner. Therefore, I will not call your parents." Ms. Carter pauses. "This time."

My whole body deflates in relief. I can feel the tension swooshing out of my neck and shoulders.

"But," Ms. Carter says, "you will stay after in my room until you have finished tonight's assignment and handed it to me." Ms. Carter turns from me, her drab, black dress swishing as she heads for her desk. "Take your seat."

Nodding, I sit and open my book, get a fresh piece of paper from my notebook, and a number two pencil to follow commandments number four and five.

The room is quiet compared to class. I can hear the faint buzz of the wall clock, the muffled sounds of students out in the hall, and the scratching of Ms. Carter's pencil at her desk. Is she allergic to pens?

I tap my pencil, bouncing the eraser against my book,

bite my lip, and look at the assignment. Graphs. This will be easy.

The clock buzz seems to get louder. It reminds me of a bee buzzing at a window, trying to get out. Like I want to get out of this room. I squirm in my seat.

Concentrate, Bly, concentrate.

Problem number one. Done. I look at the assignment again. Good. Odds only.

I stand to adjust my pants. Ms. Carter looks up. I sit before she can say anything.

Scratching my head, I look at number three. Another easy one. All I need to do is find the y-intercept.

'Why' should I find the 'y'-intercept? To get out of this stupid room. I giggle, covering my mouth a second too late.

"Is something funny Ms. Tanner?"

"No, sorry," I say, and bend my head down, trying to look serious.

I have to get this done before Mom expects me home. If I don't call in time, she'll worry. I can come up with some excuse about missing the bus.

My stomach does that flip-flop thing it always does when I think about lying.

Problem five. Y-intercept. Commandment number six; write it all down, easy or not. Easy. Done.

It takes fifteen minutes more to finish. Once I get in thinking mode, I tune out everything else.

"Done? Now that was not so bad, was it?" Ms. Carter looks at my full paper, done with a number two pencil and showing my work, and nods. "You know you could ace this class, Ms. Tanner, if you did your homework on time. As it is, you are not even passing." She sets the paper on a pile, shaking her head. "I do not understand you young people. No respect. No work ethic. . . ."

No Mathletes for me.

I want to stick my tongue out at her. I can tell I'm in for a long sermon.

There's five minutes left to make it to the office phone and call before my mom starts to wonder where I am. I can see her swerving her way around kids and toys, looking out the living room window, checking her watch again. If she calls the school, she might find out I have detention. And if they find out about detention, they might find out about my grades. And if they find out about my grades. . . .

"Um, Ms. Carter? I'm sorry to interrupt."

She looks at me with wide-eyed horror. You'd think I told her I'm planning on burning the school down. "My mom is going to worry about me."

"Oh, yes. I am sorry. You go on now."

Ms. Carter apologizing? It doesn't make sense, but whatever. I grab my bag and dash as fast as I can to the office phone.

Oh, to have a cell phone!

"Oh, hi, Bly. Is it that late already?" Mom's voice is as smooth and sweet as the icing she made the other night. "How'd you miss the bus?"

"I was, um. . ." my eyes catch another copy of a Mathletes

67

flier—in bright pink over the school secretary's desk, ". . . just talking to Ms. Carter about Mathletes," I say.

How had that come out of my mouth? I can feel my face turning red and twirl my body around to the wall so the office staff won't notice the color working its way up to my hairline. These excuses are coming out too easily.

I feel like I'm becoming someone I don't want to be. Marsha says I can only control myself, but what if I can't even control that?

"Oh, Bly, your father will be so excited. I'll come pick you up soon. Jada just messed her diaper and you know how Sarah is when I try to get her in the car seat. Wait at the door by the bus pick up. Or maybe you should start walking home. Go the bus route so I can find you. You can tell me all about Mathletes over a snack."

Hanging up, I slump down onto the nearest chair.

Most of my lies have been small excuses, but I'm feeling their weight all the way from my shoulders to my shoes.

And I'm no closer to the photography club and winning that contest than before.

Chapter 18
Friday Night Dinner

Open Mouth, Insert Spoon Bread

What's the formula for finding the area of a trapezoid?" Dad says, before shoveling some sweet potato spoon bread into his mouth. "Delicious, Mother," he mumbles with his mouth full.

"I thought you'd like it," Mom says, giving a spoonful to Jada, who grabs the spoon and shoves it into her mouth.

"Base one plus Base two, multiplied by the Height, and divided by two," I say. But most of my brain is trying to guess the price of taxes and shipping on my film to see if I'll have enough after Cherie pays me on Monday.

"Let's talk about something else," Sarah says. "This is boring."

"Ah! That's where you're wrong, Sarah. Bly and I love math. It's like solving puzzles. You like puzzles, don't you?" Dad serves himself a second helping of spoon bread.

Sarah nods. "Yes, especially if they have ponies."

"There you go, Sarah. Math."

Dad may like the sweet potato spoon bread, but Sarah doesn't seem so sure. She stirs it around and tastes it with the tip of her tongue. "Bly likes other things. Let's talk about other things. She likes pictures."

I blush, but she's given me an in. I open my mouth to say something about photography club and the contest. . . .

"How about Mason? Mason, what did you do at school today?" Mom says.

"I told you already."

"But you didn't tell Dad."

This'll take a while. They'll have to pull out one word at a time from Mason. Talking isn't his thing.

I excuse myself and clear my place. I've got half an hour before Cherie calls and I'm in charge of dishes tonight.

Chapter 19
Friday Night

How Many Kinds of Ketchup Are There?

only have a half-hour. Dad's taking me to a show." Cherie looks all fancied up on the screen in some creamsicle-colored fluffy dress and her hair piled up on her head.

"Then, let's get going," I say. "The topic is, 'Make up your own classification system for the items in your refrigerator. You must have at least three levels in this system and be able to justify your classification. Have an opening and closing paragraph.'"

"Well, I'm not by my fridge, but I kinda know what's in there," Cherie says, looking at her nails. "Okay here goes."

Cherie starts naming items and putting them in her own idea of order. She's so fast with it, I have a hard time keeping up, and my spelling is horrible. Her fridge is different than mine, including things like truffle oil, crabmeat, and five kinds of ketchup.

"Then there are the mustards. I think that should go in 'tasty add-ons' with the ketchup, but give them a sub-class of 'less calories.'"

"Mustard has less calories than ketchup?" I ask. "How do you even know that?"

"Of course. It has less sugar. I always use mustard instead of ketchup. Except on my eggs. But now I use hot sauce on my eggs. Cut the sugar whenever you can." Her dad, in a fancy suit, paces in the background. "Almost done, Daddy," she says.

He looks at his watch. "Five minutes." Then he paces out of the picture.

"Okay," I say after a few more minutes of her listing and categorizing what's in her fridge. "I think you have enough items and categories. Now you need your closing paragraph."

Cherie rattles off a decent paragraph. Why does she want my help? She knows what she's doing the whole time.

"So," she says, after her final sentence. "You'll have this typed up and emailed to me by Sunday night, right?"

"I'll print it and bring it to school," I say. "And you'll have the money on Monday?"

"Yes, I'll slip it in your locker."

"Cherie, time is up."

"Coming Daddy," she says, and the screen goes blank.

Now, I have to figure out how to spell all these things. And, maybe it isn't really cheating, since I don't do anything but play secretary. I try to make myself believe it, but I still give a little shiver.

Never, never again.

Chapter 20
Saturday

How Come Only Cinderella Has Animals Helping Her Clean?

I wake up with a smile, remembering that I'll be able to buy film soon. My fingers itch to take more pictures. I'm determined that today will be the day I tell my parents I want to join photography club instead of Mathletes. And, if that goes well, maybe I'll even tell them a little bit about my grades. Oh, and I'll get Mom to take me for fabric for my pajama pants.

I know I can bring my grades up if I just try harder.

My window is open and a nice breeze comes in, along with the sound of birds singing. Yep. Today is going to be perfect.

After breakfast, chores, and a quick lunch, I set to work cleaning and organizing my room. If I'm going to try harder, I figure that's a good place to start. Neither cleaning nor organizing is my strength, exactly, but I'm trying harder, so it has to be done.

First, I have to get an idea of what's here. I use my scientific knowledge about classification. It's mostly books, papers, clothes, and garbage. Okay, so I can make four piles, with a fifth for anything weird. I get to sorting, trying not to read every scrap of paper I find. That can come later. But I do have to stop and read the play I wrote last summer. It isn't bad. Maybe we can do it next summer. Jada will be old enough to play the dog by then. I set it on the pile with the papers.

I find the book of puzzles I'd gotten in my stocking at Christmas. It won't hurt to do one or two. After all, I've been working a good ten minutes. Who can sort for longer than that without going crazy? I hunt around for a pen. After a few minutes, I find one under my bed, behind my slippers. Jada probably put it there. Leaning back against my bed, I flip to a Sudoku puzzle and start working on it.

There's a knock on the door and it opens. "Dinner's ready, Hon. Didn't you hear me call?" Mom says.

I put down the puzzle book and the pen. "Dinner? What time is it? How did it get to be dinner time?"

"It's almost 5:30. Come on, Bly. Everyone's at the table waiting for you." She shakes her head and walks out.

Now I can hear the little guys in the background. Jada chatters away, banging her spoon. Sarah sings, and Mason makes truck noises, probably using his fork to dig into whatever food is nearby.

I jump up and head to the kitchen. Something smells good. On my way out my door, I kick a paper. Picking it up, the title on it catches my eye.

BEGINNING SEWING
ASSIGNMENTS AND DUE DATES

"Mom," I shout, as I dash down the stairs, paper clenched in my hand. "You forgot to take me to the fabric store."

Chapter 21
Saturday Evening

Fabric and Film

I run to the fabric store as the lady locks the door. "Please, please, I'll be quick," I say.

"Sorry, I'm already closing ten minutes late. My babysitter is going to kill me." She turns, walking away.

I catch her by the sleeve of her sweater. "Please. I'll do anything. My pajama project is due for school. I'll sweep your floors, I'll pay twice the price, I'll babysit your kids." I'm on my knees in front of her, the scratchy concrete from the sidewalk scraping my pants.

"Bly, what is wrong with you?" Mom comes up behind me and pulls me up by the armpits. The lady gives me a dark look and takes off into the parking lot.

"I don't know why you're acting this way," Mom says, dusting off my knees.

This is my perfect opening. My chance to tell her everything. My heart hurts so much I want to vomit up the truth. But instead, I lie.

Again.

I have to work this grade stuff out myself. I have to try harder.

My heart goes into my stomach as the lie slips off my lips. "It's just that, um, someone was telling me about the cutest material in here."

"Well, settle down. We can either wait until Monday, or go to Wal-Mart now."

"Wal-Mart," I say, re-energized. If I make the pants really fast, maybe I won't lose too many points and at least I can pass sewing class. That'll be something.

Wal-Mart is a few blocks away. It'll take longer to find a parking spot than to get there.

"You go ahead and run in," Mom says, pulling to the curb. "I'll find a place to park and meet you in the fabric section."

"Okay," I say, hopping out of the car.

The store is as crowded as I'd guessed from the parking lot. Walking up the aisle that leads to fabrics, weaving through the crowd, I see a familiar brown, over-sprayed football of hair. *Ms. Carter.*

I slip into the closest aisle—kitchen gadgets. Figuring I have a minute to kill before making sure she's gone, I work my way down the aisle, fiddling a little here and there. If I can babysit a few times maybe I can get something fancy here for Mom and Dad for Christmas. As I get near the end of the aisle, by the potholders, I hear a familiar voice.

"It was awful," someone sounding like Cherie says.

I peek through the dishcloths and see the back of what

could be Cherie's blond hair. Over her shoulder, I catch the edge of Tina's face. She giggles.

"Seriously, the look he gave me. . . ."

It is Cherie. I skooch closer, doing my best not to knock over the napkin rings near my hips.

"So what are you gonna do about it?" Tina asks.

"I don't know," Cherie says. She flips her hair and I catch a glimpse of Tina's face. I jump back, knocking over some napkin rings.

"Shoot," I say in a whisper.

What's Cherie doing at Wal-Mart? She's supposed to be in Chicago.

I run down the aisle toward can openers, hoping I'll make it around the corner before they get a look at me and know I was spying. The last thing I need is to be insulted at Wal-Mart. I'm halfway to the corner when more things clatter to the floor, but I don't stop. Slipping around the display, I run straight into. . . .

"Bly, you know not to run inside a store. What's gotten into you tonight?" Mom holds my shoulders and looks me in the eye. I notice how close I am to her height.

I take a breath. "Sorry, Mom. Um, fabric is this way." I lock my arm in hers and head toward fabric, keeping my eye out for the hair-sprayed football.

Running into Ms. Carter will not be a good idea. She and Mom haven't met, as far as I know, but I'm sure Ms. Carter would have nothing against bad-mouthing me and my grades in the middle of Wal-Mart on a Saturday night. And then telling

Mom how sorry she is about the death in the family.

"Oh, look at this fabric," Mom says, fingering something soft and silky.

It's super pretty. It's deep blue with thin squiggles of gray. I rub it against my cheek.

Umm, now that would be comfy to sleep in.

"What kind of fabric does your paper say to get?"

"Paper?"

"Don't you have a paper from class that tells you what kind of fabric to get and how much?" Mom asks.

"Well, yeah, but I, um. . . ."

Mom shakes her head. "Forgot it. Alright, we'll take our best guess." She fingers fabrics set up on a circular display. "Has anyone else brought in their fabric yet?"

I wince, feeling guilt drip like sweat from my skin. "A few people."

"And what kind of fabric did they bring?"

"Someone has one with little blue flowers on it."

"That sounds cute. What kind of fabric is it?"

I look around, touching any fabric that looks similar. "This kind," I say, feeling a red fabric, covered with trains. It's something Mason would like.

Mom feels it. "Flannel. That makes sense. Look for flannel."

Stroking fabrics, I go around the entire rack, twice. Everything is for boys or babies.

"This one's not bad," Mom says, pulling out a bolt of powder blue with pink polka dots.

"It looks like something you'd put on Jada," I say. I sigh. This isn't going well.

"Speaking of Jada, it's getting late. Pick something and let's go."

"But they're ugly."

"Sorry."

I lean against the fabrics, close my eyes and think. There has to be something cute in the store. Opening my eyes, I find myself staring at the silky fabric that caught my eye when we started. "That one."

"I think it'll be hard to sew on. It's going to slip around."

"I don't care. That's the one."

Mom sighs. "Grab it and let's go."

Now I'll have the chance to catch up in sewing. How hard can it be once you have the material? I'll pretend I'm the guy in the basement all alone sewing prom dresses.

While we wait in line at the checkout, I scan all the stuff they're hoping you'll throw in your cart without thinking: gum, magazines, film. . . FILM!

"Please hold this, Mom?" I ask.

Mom takes the material from me and I go closer to the film. Maybe I can find what I need. A gagillion different choices are before me. Actually, using my math skills, a quick scan shows there are seventeen kinds. Mine has to be one of them, but I can't remember what the packaging looks like, so I have to study each one.

Bam! There it is. The sixteenth one I look at. And it's only $28.50. I'll have money left over. But, why wait until Monday?

80

Then I'll still need to find a way to the store.

"Mom, can I borrow $30? I'll pay you back on Monday."

"Didn't we just give you some money?" Mom asks.

"Yeah, but not enough for the film. And it's right here. And cheaper than I can get online. And I. . . have the money to pay you back." I show her the box, holding it in my hand like a treasure.

Mom looks right in my eyes. "How did you manage to earn the rest of the money? You haven't done any babysitting lately."

I hold back a shiver. I should have said I found it in the back of my sock drawer, or that someone owed me money and finally paid me back. Or even that I happened upon a stranger who handed me the money and ran away. But the truth almost slips out of my mouth before I can stop it. "Cherie is paying me for. . ." I catch myself. ". . .some tutoring."

I swallow.

Mom stares.

Someone behind us in line says, "Excuse me," and pushes her way in front of us.

Mom gasps. "You and Cherie? Are friends again?" Mom's eyes get kind of watery.

"No, not exactly. More like study buddies," I say, rolling the film around in my hands, afraid if I let go of it, I'll never get it back. Cherie and I will never be friends again, after the birthday debacle. We don't talk about the birthday debacle.*

Mom plucks the film from my hands and puts it on the conveyor belt with the fabric. "I hope the tutoring leads back to a good friendship. You two were inseparable at one time."

I mumble something, grab the bag, and head to the car.

* The Birthday Debacle. Picture this: Roller Skating Rink. Me never on skates before. Me crashing into the party lady carrying Cherie's three-tiered cake. Cake meets floor, and my face. Party lady taken out on a stretcher. Now, picture Cherie's face. Yeah. It was that bad.

Chapter 22
Saturday Night To Sunday Morning

Do Not Eat the Doughnut

Lying and lying should not be the same word. They don't fit together at all. After lying to my mom, it's hard lying in bed.

I look at my clock every fifteen minutes until 4:08 am. Then, somehow fall into a deep sleep, not waking until Dad comes up to check on me.

"Hey, sleepy head. It's almost lunchtime. I snagged you the last doughnut."

As I sit up, he hands me a glass of orange juice and a doughnut that looks like too many little hands have touched it.

"No thanks on the doughnut," I say, handing it back to him. I drink the juice down without taking a breath.

From now on, no lying before lying.

Chapter 23
Sunday Afternoon

Rust and Poop

I finish the report for Cherie, print it off, and erase it from my folder on the family computer. Guilt drips from me as I find a large envelope to put it in for safekeeping.

"Never again," I whisper, as I put the envelope in my backpack.

That done, I grab Polly, now with film, and yell to mom as I head out the door. "Back in a little bit."

Things I find to take a picture of:

1) A close-up of bark with some kind of bug marks on it (it looks like a gravel construction site).

2) A balled-up piece of paper (from up close it looks like buildings in a city and it has a great shadow off to one side).

3) Smushed dog poop (No, really, it was cool, maybe my favorite).

4) A rusted part of a metal frame on a swing set.

I promise myself I'll stop at four pictures. This film needs to last a while, at least until I can come up with the money to buy more.

Heading back to the house I realize how cold it is. The wind whips my hair around and my arms are covered in goose bumps. Somehow when I'm taking pictures, I don't notice the weather.

Back home, I lay the pictures out on my bed and study them. The swing set one is okay, but you can tell it's a swing set, so I don't like that part. I like having to look really hard at something to figure out what it is. And, seriously, the smushed poop one is the coolest. I got so close when taking the picture that the smell went up my nose and all I could see was the poop. Someone must have stepped on it with a sneaker, because it looks like a tire track in mud. No one will ever guess what it really is.

I carefully place them in my nightstand drawer with the others, put Polly away, and wash my hands. I never touched the poop, but the thought of it makes my hands feel dirty.

Cherie's report done, and some great new pictures. I'm ready for a new week of school.

This will be the week I get back on track.

Chapter 24
Monday, Sewing Class

Hold Your Nose

Things Mrs. Brimhall should have covered at the beginning of the school year:

1) Silky material and beginning sewers do not go together.

2) Do not keep running a sewing machine that has jammed. It won't miraculously unjam.

3) Teachers are not happy when a sewing machine starts smoking. They will yell at you to stop sewing.

4) But you may be so flummoxed that your foot goes down harder on the petal making things worse.

5) If you do keep running said machine, prepare for smoke and stink throughout the classroom.

6) The halls are very noisy with a classroom of girls coughing, choking, and giggling.

7) Soft, blue material with grey squiggles sewn into a tangled ball will not make very good pajama pants.

8) But, in the right light, it takes a great picture.

Chapter 25
Monday, School

Out of My Hands

When I see Cherie in the hall before science class, I hand her the envelope. I'm sure everyone around me knows what's inside and I'll be found out any second. Other than taking it from me, she ignores me. I don't dare ask her about the money.

Note to self: When helping someone cheat on homework (which, BTW, will never happen again), don't forget to also do your own.

It looks as though everyone but me turns in a paper to Mr. Bines. I may have gotten my film, but at the expense of bringing up my own grades, along with lying and cheating.

Why am I making these stupid choices?

Sitting next to Porter, I feel my eyes water and purposefully pinch myself, hard, to stop the tears.

"Ouch," I say, jumping from my seat just as Mr. Bines stands, ready to start class.

"Bly," Mr. Bines says, "Did you have some kind of

announcement to make."

"No, sorry," I say, sitting again, my face bright red.

Porter looks at me with his head cocked.

I give a weak smile and pretend to pay attention to Mr. Bines.

During our lab, I can't pay attention at all. Cherie and Porter work together, with the paper in front of me staying blank. At one point, Porter grabs the paper and writes down the results.

"You doing okay, Blyster?" He asks.

"Oh, yeah, sorry," I say.

"What's bugging you?" Porter asks.

"I don't want to talk about it," I say, taking the paper back and putting much more attention than I need to on making it legible as we finish the assignment.

How can I tell him that I'd cheated? And lied? And then forgotten to do my own assignment? Smart kids don't do that. Another reason I'm a failure. Another reason I'm not the kind of kid Porter should be hanging out with. But without Porter, what would I have? He's my best friend. I can't let him find out I'm stupid.

I try my hardest to pay attention. With Porter's help, we finish right before the bell rings. He'd have been faster doing it himself. Cherie prances out of the room, giving her perfect wave to her select few. But now I know about some of the imperfect parts of her that don't show up to the rest of the school.

I find $30 in my locker at the end of the day. Holding it

makes my hands feel as if they are slimy. I can't wait to give the money to Mom.

I hope that makes me feel better.

Chapter 26
Tuesday, School

Blabitty Blah, Blah

I sulk through the school day. Everything the teachers say sounds like blabbing.

Mrs. Brimhall: Put your blab blah blabbity blab and then blah over blah blabbity blah.

Mr. Bines: Now blabbity blab lab test blabby blabbity blah.

Until I get to geography. I get there early.

"Mr. Scott, I have to be in photography club, I really have to, but my dad wants me to be in Mathletes and it meets at the same time and I can't tell him cause—well never mind that—and I really, really, really want to meet Jennifer Gardoney, she's my favorite photographer ever and please, you've got to help me, please change the day of your club so I can be in both clubs and win the contest and not get my dad mad at me cause. . . ."

Mr. Scott's hand goes up.

I stop talking and try breathing. *Inhale. Exhale.*

"Sit down, Bly. It's time for class to start. We'll talk later."

Nodding my head, worded out, I go to my seat and plop down, all energy gone.

Mr. Scott: Blabbity blah blah test blah bitty blah blah Thursdditty blah blahby blab photography blah.

My head shoots up from its resting place on the desk. Did he say he was switching the club to Thursday?

". . . as we finish our study of Europe," Mr. Scott says, turning on a power point.

Sighing, I drop my head again, turning a bit to the side so I can still see the pictures. Maybe something will excite me. . . .

Wait! I'm supposed to be working harder so I can bring my grades up, so I can be in clubs and win the contest and show I'm not a failure and I can still be Dad's little professor.

I shoot up in my seat with my eyes wide. I will pay attention or die trying.

"And our last one shows Mount Vesuvius and how it looks today. That's our reading assignment tonight—Europe, pages 153-186. And a two-page paper on any topic you'd like to cover about Europe. If you use sources other than the book, it'll count as extra credit."

Extra credit is what I need. I write down the assignment as fast as I can on a piece of loose paper in my backpack.

On my way out the door. Mr. Scott stops me. I don't want to be late for Ms. Carter again and my face must show it.

"Come after school and we'll talk about the club."

"But I have to go to Mathletes," I say.

"Clubs don't start until 15 minutes after the bell."

"Okay," I say, running away as I speak. "I'll be there."

91

Everyone's quiet as I slide into math class just before the bell. Ms. Carter is passing around papers as the bell stops ringing. Test.

I tiptoe to my seat and place my backpack under my chair, after grabbing my number 2 pencil. I'm sitting before she sees me. Ms. Carter gives the test to me upside down, like everyone else.

"You may turn your paper over and begin," she says, walking to the front of the room.

Now's my chance to bring my grade up. That'll solve half of my problems. Tests and I are good friends. I stare at the paper and point my pencil at the first problem.

The test is on trinomials. Easy. The hard part is turning off the part of my brain that wants to think about photography.

If I give in for a minute, maybe it'll stop. Then I can do my math.

I take pictures in my mind's eye. First, of the marks on my desk, from all different angles. One scratch looks like a fingernail and I think of Cherie. Then I remember how I felt doing her work and lying to Mom about it.

"ARGH," I shout, standing and shaking, all in one motion.

I freeze.

Ms. Carter stares at me like she's looking at some strange creature in the zoo.

My face burns and I sit, missing my chair, and landing on the floor.

"Ms. Tanner, to the office. And bring me your test. NOW."

I am so dead. I am so dead. So totally dead.

I stand, trying not to rub my bum, sore from landing on the edge of my seat. I glance over at Marsha. She looks like she's going to cry.

Paper in hand, backpack over my shoulder, and number 2 pencil in my back jeans pocket, I plod toward the front of the room, listening to the quiet snickers along the way.

At least I provide entertainment for the class.

Chapter 27
Tuesday, School

A Jail Sentence

Detention. A new word for me. I've had the stay-after-school-a-few-minutes that day with Ms. Carter, but this is real, live, sitting-in-a-special-room-after-school-after-Mr.-Kamai-yells-at-me detention.

All I can think of is the trouble I'm going to be in with Dad, for no good reason, other than that Ms. Carter hates me. I can't even defend myself. Every time I open my mouth, nothing but the word "but" comes out.

Mr. Kamai: Ms. Carter warned me about you.

Me: But. . . .

Mr. Kamai: She said it was only a matter of time before she had to send you here.

Me: But. . . .

Mr. Kamai: I'll let you practice sitting still in detention after school.

Me: But. . . .

Mr. Kamai: Exactly. Go sit on your butt in your next class,

then come back after school for detention.

Slinking down the hall towards gym, the bell rings as I pass math and Marsha joins me. She pats my shoulder but doesn't say anything. I can feel her support even without words and we slip through the crowd quietly until we make it to the gym hall.

I know she'll turn the opposite way I need to go at this point, but before she does, she speaks, barely loud enough for me to hear.

"I'm sorry she treated you like that." She heads away from me before I can say anything back, but it makes me smile a little.

I straighten my shoulders and march into gym class, knowing someone might believe in me.

In detention, I sit. Bells ring. I sit. People walk in and out of the room. I sit. Clubs start. I sit.

A hand on my shoulder breaks me out of my daze, but I'm not sure if I'm allowed to move.

"Bly? Let's go." Mom's voice is soft. Kind.

I fly up from my seat and into my mother's arms. "Oh, Mom," is all I can say before I start crying.

Mom hugs me tight and kisses my cheek. "Grab your stuff and let's go home."

Chapter 28
Tuesday, At Home

The Little Professor and the Mad Dad

"Detention?" Dad yells. "My daughter?"

"Lower your voice, honey, you don't need to scare everyone," Mom says.

I sit in the squishy, old plaid chair in the corner of the living room, trying not to cry. I've been in my room since coming home, not interested in dinner. Now that the little guys are in bed, it's time to face the times tables. Or, rather, the yelling.

Just, please don't take my camera away. Anything but that.

Dad takes a deep breath. "You're right. Let's start over." He sits on the footstool in front of my chair and takes another deep breath. "Okay, Professor. Let's hear your side of the story."

I look at him through wet eyes, wondering where to start. It's all such a jumble in my head and if I tell him a little, I might spill everything.

I have to solve this myself. I just have to. No one can

know how dumb I am.

"My teacher hates me." I startle myself and cover my mouth. The words have slipped out without me thinking. At least I didn't tell my secret.

"Your teacher hates you," Dad says. He looks at Mom. She shrugs her shoulders. "This is your math teacher?" he asks.

I nod.

"And why would a math teacher hate my Little Professor? I'm surprised she hasn't asked you to teach her class for her."

Here's my chance. I can spill it all. How I'm failing practically everything in seventh grade. How I want so bad to be in photography club, even if it means missing Mathletes. How the more I think about Ms. Carter leading it, the less it sounds like fun. How I want to enter the contest and meet my favorite photographer. How I'm a total failure and may as well drop out of school now and learn to be a street sweeper or something.

But that isn't what comes out of my mouth.

The part of me that can't tell, that can't bear to see the disappointment in Mom's eyes or have Dad find out I'm not his perfect little daughter, is stronger than the part of me who wants to get the truth out.

"She, she. . . . All I did was stand up during a math test. I needed to stretch for a second."

Mom speaks up. "The principal said you screamed out, disrupting the test."

"I guess I made a little noise, but I wasn't trying to bother anyone." My cheeks are wet and I sniffle and wipe my hand over the tears.

97

Mom hands me a tissue. Dad sighs and turns his back to me. His shoulders rise like he is taking another deep breath. I must be exhausting.

He turns around, facing me.

"Our children do not get sent to the principal's office. Our children know how to behave. Do you understand?"

I nod.

"You are smart enough to get along with a crabby teacher, and I expect you to do so. Mathletes will make you two get to know each other better. That should help as well. I expect more from my little professor, got it?"

He softens for the last part and gives me a kiss on the forehead.

"Now, no more reports of the principal's office."

I nod again.

"Good." Dad sits in his special chair and opens a book. "Good night, kiddo."

Mom kisses me as well. "Get to bed, honey. I'll see you in the morning."

I plod up the stairs to my room. Something in the back of my brain tries to flip me around and break the truth to them. At the top step, I stop and turn, my foot suspended over the next step down. But I can't go further. It's like there's an invisible wall stopping me. A wall filled with fear and disappointment.

I go to my room, open up my math book and grab a number two pencil.

Chapter 29
Wednesday

Knot Gonna Happen

Running off the school bus, I push my way in front of the crowd and into the school. I have to see Mr. Scott before class. He might assume I'm not interested in the photography club since I hadn't shown up after school. I can't let him think that. He has to change his mind about the day the photography club meets. I'm going to show him that I deserve to be part of the group that goes to Chicago.

"Mr. Scott, Mr. Scott," I repeat, running into the room.

He's at his desk working on something. He drops his pen and looks at me. "Good morning, Bly. How can I help you?"

"I'm sorry I didn't come after school yesterday. I, um. . . couldn't," I say. No need for him to know why.

"Oh, that's right. You were wanting me to change the club meeting date."

"Yeah. Please? I want to be a part of it so bad, but my dad wants me to be in the Mathletes."

"Oh? Are you one of those people who works out of both

sides of your brain?"

"What?"

"Our brains have one side that deals more with creative thinking, like photography, and one that deals more with logical thinking, like math," Mr. Scott says, getting up from his seat and writing something on the board.

"That's interesting and all," I say, "but can you change your club's meeting date?"

"Sorry, Bly. I can't. We had a vote yesterday, and everyone wanted to keep the club on Tuesday."

My body deflates like a balloon with a leak in it and I have to hold onto the desk to keep from falling on the floor.

I limp my deflated body out of the room and down the hall to sewing class, making it just before the bell rings.

I pick up my knotted fabric and stare at it. I'll be picking knots out for days.

Before I sit down, Marsha sits in the empty chair next to mine. "I'm done with my pants. Let me help you," she says.

"Really? But this is so boring," I say, trying to let her off the hook.

"I like picking out knots," she says. "I can pretend I'm poking at my big sister."

She laughs and so do I.

Chapter 30
Wednesday, Math Class

Ups and Downs

When I turn in my homework, Ms. Carter nods her head.

"I thought the principal's office would do you some good," she says, her lips cracking into a grimace of a smile.

All I can do is force one side of my mouth into a half-smile. It must look pretty bad.

"Are you ready to visit there again?" she asks.

"No, ma'am," I say, slinking to my seat.

She teaches a new concept. It's probably easy, but I only hear the first sentence or two before fuzzing out. I think it's the sound of everybody's books closing that brings me back. When things come into focus, she's writing our assignment on the board. I grab my pencil, which has fallen on the floor, and write the assignment down.

At least Ms. Carter isn't as observant as Mr. Scott. As long as she doesn't call on you, if your body is in the seat and quiet, that's good enough.

I stuff everything into my backpack. Several crinkled papers try to escape. Two make it to the floor. I snatch the papers and stuff them in with the rest, zipping the backpack closed so no other papers can get it in their head to escape.

Ms. Carter, with a quick "shush," gets us all to quiet for her. I look up, afraid her shush is meant only for me, but she's looking at the entire class.

"Some of you made it to Mathletes yesterday, while a few of you, whom I thought would be there, did not show up. I expect to see more of you next week. That is when we will have our entry test. Most of you in this class should have no problem with the test. But, remember, grades must also be a C or above to participate in clubs."

I wait for Marsha and we walk together to the gym hall. Maybe my life is falling apart, but it seems like I have a new friend. Of course, who knows if she'll want to be my friend when she finds out what a loser I am. Such an idiot. I won't even be good enough for an outcast like Marsha. A nice outcast, for sure, but according to Rockport Junior High society rules, definitely an outcast.

We're almost to the gym hall before she speaks. "I think you live near me. I've seen you at the park by my house a couple of times."

"Beaumont Park?"

She nods.

"How come I don't see you on the bus?" I ask.

"My grandpa likes to drive us to school," she says. "It's his excuse for stopping for his morning donuts and coffee."

"Cool. We should hang out sometime," I say as we separate.

She nods and I watch her slip down the hall. She turns with a smile and a wave before heading into her class.

I skip into the gym locker room. Her smile makes me feel maybe something is going okay in my life.

I don't know all hope will be crushed within minutes.

Chapter 31
Wednesday, Gym

Ode To Gym Class

Oh, Gym Class,

Oh, Gym Class.

You of the Volleyballs and Jocks

Of the Lockers filled with BO and Perfume

Of the open shower and stinky broken toilet.

Are you there to give us all a break

From the tedium of using our minds?

Then you should also give us a break

From having to remember our gym clothes.

Oh, Gym Class,

Oh, Gym Class.

A class where no one can fail.

Unless, of course,

You are as stupid as I am.

Chapter 32
Wednesday

A Big Fat 'A'

Leaving the smell of BO mixed with perfume behind, I step into the hall to be jostled all the way through the building to the A hallway where my regular locker is. The sounds around me pound inside my head; some jocks giving each other grief, a gaggle of giggling girls sounding like geese as they horn their way along, and a teacher yelling at her class to behave or next time she'll let them out late.

I feel so weighted down. Who fails gym? I open my locker and shove my backpack inside. It takes some stuffing, but I get it in.

"Hey, Blyster," Porter says as I close the locker door. "What did you get on your science paper?"

I stumble with what to say.

Cherie prances by. "I got an 'A,'" she says, giving me a hint of a wink.

"Well, good for you," I shout to her as she continues down the hall.

"What was that for?" Porter asks.

I look up at him and feel my cheeks start to glow. "Nothing," I say. "Just. . . good for her."

Porter shrugs and we walk to the bus together.

As the bus pulls away, Porter unzips his backpack and gets out a small notebook.

"What are you doing?" I ask.

"Going over my homework assignments," he says, making a few more marks on the page.

I shake myself out of a stare. My dad buys me a notebook each year for my homework assignments, but it's always lost the first week of school. How does someone ever remember where they put things like that? How do they remember to write their assignments down? And if they remember both of those, how do they remember to look at it later? All of that is another world to me. I'm lucky to remember to bring home my backpack. If it has the right books inside, that's a bonus. That's not even talking about remembering to do the homework, not to lose it, and to turn it in.

I look around to find my backpack. After only a moment of looking, my head goes between my knees and I let out a moan.

"What's wrong?" Porter asks, his concern sounding in his voice.

"Nothing," I say, "Only, do you know any sixth graders I can start becoming friends with?"

"Why?"

"I think I'll be seeing a lot of them next year."

Chapter 33
Thursday, School

He Knows Something

There's a new face in Mr. Scott's class. He's really cute, but almost as old as Mr. Scott. He must be close to twenty-five.

"Class, this is Mr. Newell, our student teacher. Mr. Newell spent the summer traveling in the Middle East. I asked him to bring pictures of the trip as a nice way to get to know him." He whispers something to Mr. Newell and walks towards the back of the room.

I can stand a period of looking at pictures of the Middle East. *Although, I might spend more time watching Mr. Newell.* He's way cute. The lights go out and I feel a tap on my shoulder.

"I'd like to see you in the hall," Mr. Scott says softly near my ear. I freeze. I still haven't turned in the Switzerland paper. I'll think of some excuse really fast.

"Bring your backpack," he says.

I take a deep breath, grab my things, and follow him out to the hall. My heart pounds and breathing slowly doesn't seem to help.

This can't be good.

Chapter 34
Thursday, School

Bow Wow Bowers

"Sit down, Bly," Ms. Bowers says, pointing to the chair on the other side of her desk.

I'm shaking, and have been since Mr. Scott walked me to the counselor's office. When I got into the hall he motioned me to start moving and we were walking before I knew what was happening.

"Don't worry about this," Mr. Scott said. I don't think my worry button totally turned on until he said that.

"Um. Where are we going Mr. Scott?" I asked, trying to sound casual. But my voice came out in about three different pitches.

"Ms. Bowers would like to see you." He kept up a pretty good pace and I ran every few steps to catch up with him.

"Ms. Bowers?" I asked. "The counselor?" I'd only been in her office once, and that was to get the results on our 6th grade standardized test. She seemed okay, and she complimented me on my test scores. She made sure I got into Honor's English, even though I had to beg her a little bit. I'd had the form in my backpack for a couple of weeks, scrunched at the bottom, but forgotten about it. This memory slowed down my racing heart a little, but I know you don't get pulled out of class for good things very often.

We reach the office and Mr. Scott turns me over to Ms. Bowers and disappears.

My first thought is that Ms. Bowers has amazing hair. It's light brown, cut short, and poofed in some amazing wave. No way would my hair ever do that. Not that I wanted to look like a grownup, but it's the idea that I can't do it that bugs me.

I sit down, slowly, like the chair might explode if I'm not careful.

"I'm sorry for pulling you out of class Blythe, but I'm afraid things have gotten to a precipitous point with your schoolwork." She hands a piece of paper across the desk. "Here's a copy of your progress report. Why don't you take a look with me?"

It's a question, but I don't think I have the choice of saying no. After a deep breath, I take the paper and try to focus on it. All the D's and F's show in red ink. It shouts – HERE IS SOMEONE WHO IS SO STUPID SHE CAN'T EVEN PASS GYM.

"What's going on?" Ms. Bowers asks.

"I don't know," I say, avoiding her eyes. I put my head down and peak through my fingers. "I guess I've been having a hard time."

"Your test scores show me you are very bright. In fact, this one shows you in the 99th percentile, and this other one the 93rd. Your IQ test from 5th grade shows you in the gifted area. And," she says, pushing a key on the computer and turning the monitor around so I can see it, "your grades from last year were excellent." She's looking at me with her elbow on the desk, her fingertips holding her chin. Her eyes don't give away what she's thinking.

"I guess the teachers are harder this year," I say. "Nobody will let me turn in late work. And they don't listen to my reasons why I don't have it." I want to keep going, but I know how stupid I must sound.

Ms. Bowers sighs. "Have you signed up for any extracurricular activities yet?"

"Um, not yet," I say.

"We have a policy of a C average needed to participate in any clubs."

I swallow hard.

"You know, Bly," Ms. Bowers says. "I may not have picked up on this so soon if it hadn't been for a very observant teacher of yours. He's helped me with a few people who are struggling."

Mr. Scott. *I knew it.*

"I'm going to give you a copy of this report and I want you to get it signed by your parents. Then, I expect you to bring these grades up immediately or we'll need to schedule a conference with them." She turns her computer back towards her. "I went to bat for you for your English class, don't think I've forgotten. You can do better than this. Show me."

I take the paper and slink out of her office.

Chapter 35
Thursday, School

Stinky Switzerland

I walk down the hall, past the cafeteria, heading back to Geography. The air smells like sour milk, and I wonder if someone threw up.

I feel like throwing up.

Mr. Scott betrayed me. I thought he was the one teacher who might understand. And instead, he's ratted me out to the school counselor.

How am I supposed to get out of this?

As I pass a bulletin board, a Mathletes flier falls at my feet.

I stomp on it and keep walking, hoping I'll come up with some way of putting my life back together, the way it was in sixth grade.

By the time I get to Mr. Scott's class, I haven't come up with anything. Not unless I can somehow have extra time. Time no one else has. Like a magical time-turner.

The door is closed and the lights are still out. I hear the student teacher talking. Will Mr. Scott notice if I don't come back in? Will he think I'm still with the counselor? Here's my chance to have the time I need.

There's probably twenty minutes, maybe more, left in the period. If I can go somewhere and write this stupid geography report and turn it in before I go home, I can show Mr. Scott. I can show him I'm not as dumb as he thinks I am and I don't need him meddling in my life. I can look him in the eye with a hard stare. I won't have to say a word and he'll know. He'll know he's done me wrong by tattling on me to the counselor.

I peek over my shoulder to make sure no one's watching and run down the hall.

I know right where to hide. The bathroom in the girl's gym locker always has one stall with a clogged toilet. And the toilets have lids. It'll be quiet until class ends, and there's good light.

The halls are empty and I have no problem sneaking into the stall I want. With the lid down, it doesn't stink too badly. I can stand it for a little while.

I've always thought skipping class would be hard to do, but this is easy!

It's meant to be.

Putting my backpack on the floor, I open it and find the notebook where I've started my report. It's gotten wet from something and all the words are smeared. Time for a new page.

Ripping out a paper, I put my name and the class in the right-hand corner of the page. Now, what's the assignment? Something about a country in Europe.

I dump my backpack out onto the tiles, hoping the floor

isn't too covered in cooties. A few papers catch a breeze and try to float out of the stall area.

I grab them and get them into my backpack as fast as I can. Time is racing on and I haven't started yet. Things are still quiet in the locker room, but there's no time for neatness.

Math book, check. Stuff it in.

English, in.

Sewing notebook, stuffed.

Geography notebook. Here we go. I sit down again, feeling the seat shift a little. The smell sneaks out and I try not to gag as I flip through the pages looking for the assignment. I know I've at least taken some notes. Hopefully, this assignment is something I've written down.

Most of what is written are doodles. But everybody does that. One of the doodles is really cool. It looks kind of like a rocket ship but turned into some kind of weird looking dog. Now, if I take this pen and continued this line. . . .

NO. Stop it, Bly. I shake my body, starting at my head and going to my feet. *Concentrate.*

The shaking sends toilet stink up into my nose again. I try to ignore it and go back to looking through my notes.

Nothing. No wonder I missed the assignment.

Who am I kidding? I would probably have forgotten it anyway.

Okay, so I have to rely on my memory. It's two pages, I remember that. We're studying Europe. The class is geography.

TWO PAGES ON THE GEOGRAPHY OF A EUROPEAN COUNTRY!

I start scribbling as fast as I can. We've discussed Switzerland and its mountains in class and I've been so interested I've looked up more on the Internet at home. Two pages will be easy.

As I'm near the bottom of the second page, I hear footsteps and voices. Grabbing the rest of my papers, I stuff everything in my backpack and try to zip it closed. My heart races like crazy. If the teacher catches me here, she'll know I'm ditching class. No one uses this bathroom, except for gym class; it's too far from everything else.

I grab the handle to open the door and that's when I remember. The other reason this toilet isn't used is that the door handle sticks.

I'm dead.

Around the corner from the bathroom area, lockers clang, and girls giggle. I smell the familiar mix of BO and perfume. It's pretty much a gag fest. A few girls run past me and into the showers. Moments after they pass, I hear the water hitting the tiles and hear the echoes of the girls in there. Unlike Smithfield Junior High, in the next town, we still have a big group shower. Another reason I hate gym. The steam drifts into the bathroom. Just what my hair needs. Great.

I try jiggling the handle again. Still stuck. Then I hear a familiar, perfect voice. One with long, blond hair attached. Cherie. It's one of the voices echoing in the shower.

"The way you can tell if someone is really beautiful is if they're still beautiful when they're bald." She giggles.

Another voice speaks, but it's totally garbled over the

115

sound of the water.

"Like my aunt, when she got cancer. She could still be a big-time model," Cherie answers.

The pipes squeal as they turn off the water. It won't be long before they pass right by the bathroom stalls.

I go back to jiggling the handle. It doesn't budge. I want to get out of there before Cherie sees me. I'm not up to hearing anything rude from her. Besides, I need to get to math class.

I'll have to squeeze under the door. Kneeling, my knee hits a wet spot.

Gross. I don't even want to know what that is.

Getting down on my elbows, I start doing an army crawl. I've gotten my butt under the door when I see two sets of feet pass. Looking up I catch eyes with Cherie. She stares, then shakes her head and walks on as if I'm not there.

"Freak," says Tina, as she passes by behind Cherie.

I stick my tongue out at them both, reach under the stall for my backpack and pull.

Next thing I know, I am running out of there like I've got a timed experiment about to explode down the hall. The first bell rings as I come around the corner by the cafeteria. I make it to my seat in math a full ten seconds before the late bell.

I've done it!

I've skipped class without anyone finding out, I've gotten my report done for Mr. Scott, and I've made it to math class on time. Go me!

I just wish the sinking feeling in my stomach would go away.

116

Chapter 36
Thursday, Bus Ride Home

My Only Choice

I drop the note onto Cherie's lap without anyone but her seeing the pass. I'm getting good at this, even though it makes me feel like the tar on the road ahead of us, being smushed by the big roller truck. The bus goes around the long way to avoid the closed road. I'm glad because it gives Cherie time to answer me before she gets off.

As she walks past me at the corn stand, I feel something drop onto my lap and I cover it with my hand and stuff it in my pocket before Porter can notice.

Once Porter gets off the bus, I look around. No one sits near me. Asteroid is singing to his music. I'm safe. Pulling the paper out of my pocket, I open it up to see what she's written. But it's like she's written in another language. I turn the paper around a few different ways and squint. It looks like this:

I clal u

I stick the paper in my pocket as Asteroid pulls up to my stop.

Maybe it's in code and I can figure it out in my room.

Chapter 37
Thursday, Home

A Swinging Good Time

As I walk in the door, I hear Mason and Sarah fighting. Mom yells at them to be quiet and I can tell everyone is having a bad day.

"I know you just got home, hun, but would you please take these two to the park to run off some energy?" Mom asks, wiping her head and getting something sticky from her hands into her hair.

Knowing I can use any positive parent points I can get, I say yes. I set my backpack by the stairs and open the fridge while hoping my voice carries to Mason and Sarah. "Grab your shoes, guys, and let's go to the playground!"

They drop the toy they're fighting over and run for their shoes.

"I need help," Sarah yells.

I grab an apple and head to the front door to get her shoes on the correct feet.

"Let's go!" I say and they barrel out the door and down

the street.

They make it to the playground before I take more than one bite of my apple. Sarah jumps on the rocking duck and Mason finds a stick and digs in the sand. I sit on a swing and watch. The weather is a little breezy and cool but just right for spending time in the park. I take a deep breath and smell mayonnaise. The wind must be coming from the mayonnaise plant a few miles away.

It always feels like the smell of mayonnaise will bring good luck soon. I sure need it. I cross my fingers on the hand not holding the apple.

"Hi, Bly."

I turn around on the swing and see Marsha. She's still wearing her dress from school. I don't think I've ever seen her wear jeans. I guess I haven't changed either, but I started the day with jeans. "Hi!" I say and point to the swing next to me.

She comes around, dusts off the seat, and sits. Her legs are longer than mine and her feet drag a bit.

"Do you want to switch swings?" I ask. "Mine is a little higher."

"No thanks," she says. "I like kicking my feet around in the sand." She does little half twirls and her braid flips back and forth.

"How long since you've cut your hair? I bet it would go to your waist if it wasn't in the braid." I say. I glance at Sarah who has switched animals and is now rocking on the whale.

"I've never cut it," Marsha says. "My grandparents like it long. I kind of want to cut it sometimes."

"I think it's cool," I say. "Mine probably wouldn't look good if I grew it more. It gets frizzy and thin on the ends."

We stop talking and pump our feet and swing. Sarah and Mason play together in the sand. That might mean a fight will start soon. I hope not. I like getting to know Marsha.

I peek over and watch her hair swing as she slips back and forth. I get an idea.

"Do you mind watching Mason and Sarah for a minute?" Since we're the only ones on the playground, she can tell who I'm talking about. "I'm gonna run home for a second. I'll be fast."

She gives me a funny look, but nods, and I run to the house, shouting to the kids at the same time. "I'll be right back, guys."

In the house, I throw away my apple core, grab Polly from her pocket, and shout to Mom. "We're fine, Mom. We'll be out for a bit longer."

I don't get an answer, but she might be in the laundry room or something. She can always come to the porch and call us if she's worried.

Back at the park, I catch my breath, and Marsha talks before I can tell her my idea.

"Your camera," she said. "What are you going to take a picture of?"

"You," I say.

"Me? I'm kind of a mess right now," she says, pushing some strands of hair behind her ears.

"Don't worry," I say. "No one will know it's you."

She jumps off her swing and comes over to me, giggling. "Show me what you mean."

I haven't talked much about my photography to anyone, so I worry she might think it's weird. But I also know she won't say anything even if she thinks that.

"Let me see your braid," I say, and she swings the end of it around and hands it to me. The braided part feels soft but the ends are kind of jaggity.

Sarah and Mason notice my camera, or at least something more interesting than what they were doing, and come to watch.

This is the first time I've had an audience when I take a picture. It fills my stomach with bubbles. But I don't feel scared. It's more like excitement. Like I'm about to perform a magic trick and my audience has no idea what to expect.

I drag Marsha around the playground by the braid and she follows me, giggling. The perfect background is here somewhere.

Not the logs. We try the metal slide. Nope, and not the painted animals, either.

Sarah speaks up. "What about the sand? It's the same color as her hair—brownie tannyish."

"That's just right. Thanks," I say, and Sarah claps her hands.

"I was going to say the sand," Mason says. "But I thought she wanted to figure it out herself." Mason sticks his tongue out and I know I have to say something before they start fighting.

"Hey guys, I need your help!" They both look up at me

and I think this will work. "See that spot right there, with both sun and shadow, sweep it clean from leaves and sticks and make it as flat as you can."

"I'm going to take out the bottom part of your braid, okay?" I ask.

Marsha nods.

I hand her the hair elastic and undo the bottom six inches of her braid.

"Lay down this way with your head here." I point to the spot and hold her hair so I can lift it over her head.

Mason goes back to digging, but Sarah jumps up and down, watching what we're doing.

I lay her hair out straight on the ground, over her head. It isn't really straight, the braid has left it with a bunch of 's' curves. I stare at it for a moment and then I know what to do. Using my fingers like a comb, I follow the curves in her hair and comb through the sand.

"What are you doing," Marsha asks.

"Don't move," I say. "You'll see soon."

I run my hands through her hair and the sand a few more times until it looks just right. I get my camera ready and wait for the sun to come out from behind a cloud.

The cloud moves and the sun shines on half of her hair. I angle down, being careful not to create my own shadow.

Snap! I've got it.

"You can get up now," I say, holding the developing picture in my hand.

Marsha scuttles up and everyone gathers around to see

the picture. Now my bubbly stomach has changed, like I might throw up. I close my eyes, purse my lips and breathe out. 100, 94, 88. Breathe in. 82, 76, 70.

"Ohh," I hear, coming from more than one person. I open my eyes and look. Sarah and Marsha are smiling. Mason's head blocks my view, so I pull the picture up where I can see it.

Then I'm smiling.

"It looks like something I saw in a Japanese store at the mall," Marsha says. "The Zen garden, where you rake the sand. It's supposed to make you feel peaceful."

"Cool," I say. Before I can think of what to say next, Marsha touches me.

"Tag, you're it," she says and jumps onto the log structure and runs down the length of it, jumping easily onto the second log structure several feet away.

I take off after her and only catch up when her shoelace comes undone, and she stops to tie it.

Mason and Sarah join in the chase and after a few minutes, we all sit on one of the lower logs and catch our breath.

Sarah starts wiggling and I know what that means. "We've gotta go," I say to Marsha, as I stand and pick Polly up from next to my feet.

I hand the picture to Marsha and she looks at me like she isn't sure why. "It's for you," I say. "Thanks for letting me experiment with your hair."

Marsha smiles the biggest smile I've ever seen, gives me a wave, and skips away.

"Come on, guys," I say. "Let's go home."

123

Chapter 38
Thursday, Home

The Cheat Is On

Bly, the phone is for you," Sarah says after opening the door to my room. "Mommy said to use the phone in her room 'cause the mixer is loud."

"Okay," I say, jumping off my bed and heading to my parent's room. *What does Porter want and why is he calling before five?* His mom usually keeps him studying until then.

The mixer is loud so I close the door to my parent's room. I jump on the bed and grab the phone from the night-stand.

"Hello?" I say, expecting to hear Porter's voice.

Instead, I hear a perfectly pretty voice. "Hi, Bly. I said I'd call. Is this a good time? Are you by yourself?"

So THAT'S what the note says.

Is that why she wants me to write for her?

"Um, yeah. I'm alone." I peek in the closet to make sure Mason isn't hiding in there. He can be quiet when he's taking something apart.

All clear.

"So, what is it you want me to sign?" Cherie says, as if she's asking for the time of day.

My stomach does the wibbly-wobbly thing it's doing more and more. It's different from the bubbles earlier. I don't think counting will help. I take a deep breath and say what I need to say. "My progress report. I can't let my parents see it."

"You? Miss Smarty Pants?" I hear what sounds like a giggle covered with a hand.

I stay quiet, wanting to die inside.

She speaks again. "How about trading it for a Geography report? I got an extra day out of Mr. Scott, telling him our printer is out of ink. My country is Scotland. And you do the work. A forged signature is worth much more than $30."

Again, I stay quiet. It'll be harder to justify it as not cheating this time.

Am I really that desperate? I think about Dad's face if I show him my progress report. I see him shaking his head slowly like he's heard of a friend dying. I think about my mom and see tears coming down her face. I think of Marsha looking at me as if she doesn't know me. I think about Porter finding out how stupid I am and deciding never to sit by me again, on the bus, or in science class.

Or anywhere.

Is it worth it?

Then I remember I'm only buying time. I'll bring my grades up. Somehow, I will. It's just a matter of trying harder.

"Are you still there?" Cherie asks.

125

"Um, yeah," I say.

"Is it a deal?" she asks.

I take another deep breath. You'd think I'm some kind of yogi by now with all this deep breathing.

"It's a deal," I say.

I'm buying time, I reminded myself.

"Okay. Can you get someone to drive you in early? We can meet by our lockers. Bring your progress report and my paper for Mr. Scott."

"Deal," I say.

I hang up and realize my shirt is soaked with sweat and my heart is beating so hard I can almost see it through my wet shirt.

Cheating is better exercise than gym class.

Chapter 39
Friday Morning, School

Clicking Heels

The halls are empty and my sneakers squeak all the way to my locker. I hear early morning orchestra playing down the hall and around the corner. I hope they don't have a concert soon. The violin squeals hurt my ears.

Cherie isn't here yet and I slide my back down my locker until my bum hits the floor and put my head in my hands.

What am I doing?

Will I be a criminal after this?

Is it too late to change my mind?

I hear the click, click, click of heels coming towards me. It sounds like Mrs. Brimhall. Maybe I can hand the geography report to her and tell her what I'm planning. Then maybe she'll break things to my parents and maybe I can still hide my grades from Porter and maybe. . . .

The shoes stop in front of me. I peek at them, not able to lift my head. They're red with a sparkly band across the front. A little bright for Mrs. Brimhall.

"Let's do this before everyone else gets here." Cherie, wearing a red skirt and white blouse, stands over me, pulling a pen out of her purse. Her nails, also red, are as perfect as she is.

But now I think I know her secret. Her brain, just like mine, has a problem. I can't think straight and she can't write straight. Were we doomed to this symbiotic cheating relationship forever?

Mr. Bines would be proud of me for knowing how to use symbiotic.

But I can never tell him.

"Would you please get off the floor and let's do this!" Cherie starts to lose her cool.

I stand, open my backpack, pull out her report and hand it to her. Then, I dig deeper, looking for my progress report for her to sign.

I slip to the floor on my knees, still digging for the paper for her to sign. The sounds around me change. Instead of off-key violins, I hear footsteps and voices getting closer and louder.

"You're impossible," Cherie says, stepping around me and walking down the hall.

Books and papers are strewn across the floor, and I still can't find the one most important paper. I gather things up as quickly as I can, almost tripping a couple of people as they come down the hall. The last paper I find, with a rip and a footprint on it, is my progress report. I sit down in the middle of the floor, holding it, so relieved, I can barely move.

Then my eye catches something. It's a ripped-up candy

wrapper, but from the right angle, it might look like a mountain.

I fold the progress report and put it in my pocket, bend down and scooch forward until my eyes are inches from the wrapper.

The sound of "click, click, click" comes both through my ears and through my chin, which is on the floor.

Cherie is back!

I jump up, excited to get my paper signed. "I've got it right here," I shout as I stand, pulling the paper from my pocket.

It's Mrs. Brimhall. And walking with her is Marsha.

"What have you got, Blythe?" Mrs. Brimhall asks, reaching for the paper in my hand.

I stuff the paper back in my pocket as fast as I can. "Nothing," I say. "I thought you were someone else."

Marsha looks at me like I've grown an extra ear on top of my nose and I look away.

"Well, as long as you're here early, why don't you come down to the sewing room and work on those pajama pants of yours."

She guides me gently with her hand and I follow along, afraid to do otherwise. Marsha comes with us.

"I can help," she says.

"Your fabric is very pretty," says Mrs. Brimhall, "but as you've learned, it's difficult to sew on. If you have the knot picked out, I can show you a trick or two to keep the fabric from slipping so much."

129

Chapter 40
Friday Science Class

The Pass

When Cherie walks into class, my first instinct is to run up, hug her, and hand her the paper to sign. I manage to stop myself after taking one step. I turn around and sit on the lab stool and try to act casual.

"What was that?" Porter asks, his eyebrows almost meeting in the middle as he furrows his brow.

"Nothing," I say. "Just. . . thought of something and. . . changed my mind." One less lie to keep track of.

Cherie clicks over to her seat across the lab table from me. It's the first time I can remember she doesn't give me the sniff of disapproval as she passes. But she also doesn't look at me.

How am I going to get my paper signed? I want to turn it in by the end of the day so Ms. Bowers doesn't call home. I pull it from my pocket and hold it in my hand. There'll have to be a moment when I can pass it to her without anyone else noticing.

As we start the lab, Porter goes to the front of the room

to get our equipment. I look at Cherie. She gives a lift of the chin and I pass the paper to her. She has it signed and back to me and I shove it into my pocket before Porter makes it back to the table.

My stomach jolts again. How long am I going to feel like this?

I have to bring my grades up fast, or I'll never feel like eating again. And I've never had a secret from Porter. He's the most honest friend I have and now I'm keeping dark, dirty secrets behind his back.

But it has to be this way.

For now.

This will be over soon, I'm sure of it.

I just have to work harder.

Chapter 41
Tuesday, After School

I Scream, You Scream

I skip past Ms. Carter's classroom and wind through the halls until I get to Mr. Scott's room. If I'm going to win this contest and meet my favorite photographer, I need to learn some skills.

But the truth is—the deeper I get into cheating and lying, the less I feel like holding my camera, let alone taking pictures.

I also ignore that my parents are going to assume I'm at Mathletes.

It always feels like I'm carrying a big ball of wax around in my stomach anyway. So what's one more thing?

Mr. Scott turns from the board as I enter the room.

He glances at me and winks before he speaks to the group. "To be an official member of this club, and attend any field trips, you must have a 'C' grade point average. I'm sure you're all aware of that. But I don't take attendance, and it doesn't matter to me who comes into my classroom during this hour. So, I'll leave it at that." He sits on his desk. "Today, we're taking a look at composition."

I take more notes in this hour than in any class I've ever had. And, tonight, I'll practice what I learn. . . after I do my math homework and some make up time for gym.

Mom picks me up after club time. Before the van door opens, I hear the three little guys yelling. Sarah and Mason chant "Ice cream, ice cream" and Jada babbles along in time.

"How was school today, sweetie?" Mom shouts over the chanting.

"Fine," I say. "Some homework." I decide that admitting to homework is one way to help me make sure I get it done. Part of my plan to work harder.

"How was Mathletes?" Mom says as she pulls out of the parking lot.

Now it's time to start dodging. The noise from the backseat makes for great cover. "Fine. Did you promise these guys ice cream or something?" I ask.

"I promised after we picked you up, we'd stop for a gallon at the store for," she raises her voice and turns her head so they will hear, "after dinner."

"Drop me off and I'll pick it up," I say. This will earn me brownie points, and maybe get things off track enough that Mom will forget to ask me more. I turn to face the little guys. "What kind do you guys want?"

"Strawberry."

"Rocky Road."

"No, strawberry."

Jada adds her thoughts, "Ba, ba, ba, ba."

"Okay," I say. "I'll get Baba ice cream. How does that sound?"

"No," say Sarah and Mason.

Mom pulls up to the front of the store and gets out some cash for me. "Go ahead and get two half gallons. One of each."

I nod and go inside for ice cream.

Maybe I avoid more questions about Mathletes, but I almost bump right into Ms. Carter. Why does she have to shop at the same places we do?

"Well, Ms. Tanner. I expected to see you today after school, although I'm not sure your grades will allow club activity."

I look around to make sure Mom hasn't followed me in. "Yeah, I, um, wasn't sure I was allowed," I answer. May as well give her what she expects.

"As I said before," she continues, not giving time to hear my answer. "You could be doing very well in my class if you didn't have such poor study skills. Young people these days. . . ."

I shoot out an answer, hoping to get away fast. "Yes, ma'am. I'm trying to improve. I'll do better," I say, backing away and turning to run.

As she heads out of the store, I hope she won't see Mom. They haven't met, but everyone says that I'm a mini mom, so Ms. Carter will know right away who she is.

Snatching some ice cream, I check out as quickly as I can. Through the door, it looks as though Mom and Ms. Carter are at opposite sides of the parking lot.

I breathe out the breath I'm holding and head to the door with Strawberry, Rocky Road, Bubblegum Crunch, 62 cents change, and a head full of ideas to keep the conversation off Mathletes.

Chapter 42
Friday, Science Class

Group Schmoop

To finish up our section on Classification, or Taxonomy, we have a group project due Monday. Each table has an envelope on it with twenty items listed. As a group, each table will categorize the items in tree form, two distinctly different ways, then write a two-page report as to why you categorized them the ways you did, and what works well and doesn't work well in each system." Mr. Bines paces the room. "I want to see real thought put into this. The table with the highest score will receive a coupon for free cupcakes at Dolly's Dainties. You may use the rest of the period to begin."

Turning around to face our table, I see Porter reaching for the envelope. Cherie sits prim and pretty but somehow grabs the envelope before Porter. Porter looks as surprised as I feel. She holds it, letting it swing in her hand. "Porter, you do the classification. Bly and I will write the paper."

"But, I think he wants us to discuss everything and work as a group," Porter says, pushing up his glasses.

"He wants it done as a group," Cherie says. "He doesn't care who does what part. You want to win, don't you? This division will help us do that."

Porter and I look at each other. I shrug my shoulders. I'm not crazy about writing a paper with Cherie, and have no idea why she wants to write with me, but the prize sounds cool and maybe she's right.

"Okay. I'll have the systems set up by noon tomorrow. We can meet then, I'll answer any questions, and you guys have the rest of the weekend to finish. Sound good?" Porter takes the envelope and sticks it in his backpack.

"Sure," I say. "Where should we meet?"

"How 'bout at the swings in the park by your house?" Cherie says.

"Okay. Can you come over after that to write the paper?" I ask as the bell rings and we gather our things.

"Oh, something like that," Cherie says, swinging her purse and prancing out of the room.

Chapter 43
Saturday, Noon

The Swing Shift

I grab a light jacket and head out the door, after telling Mom where I'm going. Again, she's excited that Cherie and I are talking.

If she only knew the truth.

Porter is there already, swinging on the middle swing.

"Hey," I say, climbing onto the swing on his right.

"Hey," Porter says, continuing to swing.

I kick myself into the strongest and highest swing I can manage. Being up in the air with the wind rushing by and the landscape whizzing around me, I can almost forget what a mess I'm in. I can take all my lies and cheats and bad grades, roll them into a ball, and throw them up into the clouds, hoping they'll never come back.

It makes me feel almost good for the first time in weeks.

Slowing down a little, I pull Polly out of her pocket. What will the world look like with movement that stops forever as one blur? I kick gently, not wanting to go so fast that I drop

Polly. I take the picture up near the top of my arch, aiming towards the trees to my right. As the paper whirs out the bottom, I slow and watch the picture show up.

It's blurred, as I expect. It probably isn't going to win an award, but I decide to name it. My first named picture; "Bly's Blurry Life."

Things are going by in a blur and I don't feel in control. But, at the same time, I feel like I'm stuck without a choice. I know I'm making excuses, and almost believing them. But the itch of not believing is getting harder and harder to scratch. Can I bring my grades up before my parents find out? Is all this lying and cheating worth it? It has to be.

It just has to be.

I stop my swing and flap the picture a bit to make sure it's dry before I put it away.

Porter stops his swing. "Can I see your picture?"

I hold it to my body. I haven't shown my pictures to many people. And this one is blurry on purpose. I wasn't trying to make it good, I was trying to somehow show my confused thoughts. What if, somehow, through this picture, Porter can read my mind and know how messed up my thoughts are? Or, what if he laughs at it? Will he be laughing at me?

A car door slams behind us and I'm saved by Cherie's voice as she comes closer. "Ready to get started?" she asks, coming up behind us. I slip Bly's Blurry Life into my jacket pocket, safe from Porter's eyes.

"Let's do this at the picnic table," Porter says, heading over to the nearest one. It's in the sun, which feels great after being chilled swinging in the shade.

It takes a few minutes for Porter to show and explain the choices he's made for his two classification systems. I really like his choices. Maybe Cherie's right, and this is the best way to split things up.

"So, if you have any questions, just call. I should be home building my P39 rocket the rest of the day." Porter hops on his bike and takes off. It clatters and clunks a bit, probably a hand me down from his big brother.

I watch him until he's a speck, and wonder if I'll ever be able to stop lying to him.

"Do you want to go back to my house to get this done?" I ask. "Mom will probably make us a good snack while we work."

Cherie's face goes into the smug garbage-smelling face I haven't seen for a while. "You do it and put my name on it," she says, reaching in her pocket and pulling out her cell phone. "Mom's taking me shopping. I'll owe you a favor."

She dials while I stare, mouth open. I probably look like one of those ugly bottom-dwelling fish, but I can't get my lower jaw to raise up and connect with the upper part.

"Mommy, I'm ready to go. . . okay, see you in a minute."

I shake a little bit of sense into my head and try to talk. "But. . ." I say.

Cherie walks away without looking back.

I take a deep breath and chase her. "I don't get it. What are you saying?"

"I'll try again, since you're obviously dense." She turns and looks me straight in the eyes. "You. Write. The. Report.

You'll get us the better grade, and you know it."

She turns back and walks to the curb. Her mom's car is down the block. I only have a few more seconds to stop this from happening.

"I don't just cheat on a whim," I say. "I don't like this."

"You'll do it," she says, her hand on the car door handle. "And, you'll want something later. I'll owe you. I'm doing you a favor." And with that, she opens the door and steps into the car.

I stand there with my mouth open, feeling like she is an unsolvable math problem. It's a feeling I don't get very often and I don't like it one bit. I stare at her car as it takes off down the street. What do I do now?

Then I hear a voice.

"Hi, Bly," Marsha says. "I thought you and Cherie were doing your science report this afternoon."

Before I can answer, Sarah comes out of the house and calls to me. "Hurry home, Bly. I want to play with you." A big chilly wind whips her hair around and I imagine goosebumps on her bare arms.

"I'm really sorry, I gotta go," I say to Marsha.

I run home, my mind swirling like the wind.

Chapter 44
Tuesday, Clubs

The Contest Rules

I decide to show up at the beginning of Mathletes to see what's going on. That way, I can make up something better when Mom asks. Mom will get to me before I can get to Porter for information, and the ice cream diversion won't work every week.

I slip in and sit by Porter and Marsha, towards the back, behind a big kid. I hope it'll hide me from Ms. Carter so she won't kick me out. It'll be harder to leave without being noticed, but I'd rather leave on my own than be kicked out by Ms. Carter because my grades aren't high enough.

"Hey," Porter whispers, looking like he's afraid he'll get called out. "What are you doing here?" No talking even in clubs. Sounds like Ms. Carter.

"Just checking things out," I say.

"Here is the information for our Parent's Night on Thursday. I am sure everyone's parents will be there," Ms. Carter drones from the front of the room as she passes the papers out.

My eyebrows go up and I look from Porter to Marsha. "Parent's night?" I ask.

"Yeah, my parents are coming. Are yours?" Porter says. Marsha nods.

"Uh," I whisper, reaching for the paper from the big guy in front of me, "probably not. See ya!" I do my best to pull a disappearing act as I sneak out of the room. The stuff on this paper will give me plenty to talk about. Too much, in fact. Maybe I'll throw it away to make sure my parents don't know about it. I'll make up something for Mom.

I don't want to miss any more of photography club.

Today is the day for passing out papers. When I get to Mr. Scott's room, he's passing them out and talking about the contest.

Finally! This is what I've been waiting for. I sit in the first empty seat I notice, take a paper, and pass the rest back.

"As you can see, any middle school student in the state may enter the contest, with a five-dollar entry fee. However, our school trip to the gallery opening may only be attended by eight students; all of whom must be members of the club and must have entered the contest. That's what will fit in the school van. If we have more than eight interested in going, we'll draw straws." Mr. Scott does a half-sit on the front of his desk. "You can check out the paper for dates and other information. The contest is asking for six pictures with a theme. So, today, we'll talk about what it takes to have a theme or story in pictures."

Listening hard I don't take any notes, but everything

goes from his mouth into my photographer's heart, or eye, or whatever it is in my body that holds that stuff. It's more than holding it in my brain, because I get it on some other level, some deeper level that mixes all those organs, heart, eye, brain, together.

"So, this isn't homework, because there won't be a grade, but your assignment is to bring in six pictures with a theme. You may end up using these pictures to enter with, or you may use them as practice. See you next week!"

Everyone chats as they leave. I try to get to Mr. Scott before anyone else. I have to push through a couple of kids, but I make it.

"Mr. Scott?" I ask.

"Yes, Bly?"

I look around to make sure no one can hear me. "This rule about our grades being high enough before we can join? When do you measure that?"

"What do you mean?" Mr. Scott asks, putting away some papers.

"I mean, I can't quite join right now, cause, well, you know," I say, looking down at the floor, "but when will you decide who can go on the field trip?"

"We'll have to make that decision in two weeks."

"Two weeks. Thanks," I say, running out of the room.

I stop at my locker to make sure I have the books I need for any homework and run out of the school as fast as I can to meet Mom.

Running across the wet grass, I see someone else walking

in front of me to the same car. High-top sneakers, jeans a bit too short, in need of a good haircut. "Porter!" I call.

He turns around and waits for me. "Your mom is driving me home today."

"Oh, cool," I say.

What I should have said was, "Don't say anything about anything." But since I'm still not used to this lying thing, I don't.

Chapter 45
Tuesday, After School

She Was Right—I Thought of Something

So, how was Mathletes?" Mom asks as she pulls into traffic.

"It was great," Porter says. "We've got a parent night on Thursday."

I look at Porter, mortified.

He didn't just say that, did he?

"Oh, how wonderful!" Mom says, taking a peek at us in the mirror. "We'll be there, for sure."

"Why would you. . . ?" Porter begins.

I cut him off as quickly as I can. "That's great. It'll be fun."

Porter looks at me like I'm growing seaweed out of my ears. I smile and put my finger to my lips, making sure Mom can't see me from her angle.

Porter stays silent.

The whole car stays silent, except for some quiet humming from Mom.

At Porter's house, I offer to get Mason, Sarah, and Jada

from inside. I need a chance to explain things to Porter. At least I can tell him some of the truth.

"What was that about? Why are your parents coming to parent's night when you aren't in Mathletes?" Porter says on the way to his front door.

I turn for a quick peek to make sure Mom's car window is up. "Because they think I'm in Mathletes," I say, looking for any sign of sympathy in his eyes.

"Why?"

"Because Dad's a bit of a freak about math and I, well, I couldn't tell them how much more I wanted to go to photography club."

"Oh, man. Sorry to put you in a mess," he says, fumbling for his key.

"It's okay. You didn't know. I haven't," I hesitate, "I haven't wanted to talk about it." Or much of anything else to anyone, I finish to myself.

The door opens and Sarah jumps into my arms, with Mason stepping out after her. Mrs. Porter is behind them, holding Jada.

*****

I close the door to the study and look behind the curtain and in the closet, to make sure Mason isn't hiding anywhere. After finding Cherie's number on the caller ID, I call, fanning myself to stay calm.

She answers on the third ring.

"I'm ready for your help. I need it right away." I'm whispering, still sure someone will overhear me.

"I told you you'd think of something," Cherie says. "Hang on a sec."

I hear a door close on her side.

"Okay," she says. "Spill."

"I need to know how to fake sick," I say. I'd thought for hours about how to solve the Parent's Night dilemma. From the moment Porter spoke in the car, my mind has been churning. Faking sick is the best solution.

The only solution.

"Easy. Details." Cherie says. She sounds as calm as if she's giving fashion advice on the bus.

What kind of world am I living in and how can I get myself out?

"My parents think I'm in Mathletes and they can't find out I'm not. They plan on going to the Parent's Night on Thursday." My whole body is shaking, even my teeth are chattering.

If this keeps up, I won't need a sick excuse.

"Best thing is throwing up and a fever. Not too high a fever or they'll take you to the doctor. Tina once tried to fake it and got the thermometer to read 110. They rushed her to the hospital. If you want this to work, you have to totally follow my instructions, or I won't be responsible for the outcome."

I nod my head, but realize she can't see it. "Got it."

"It usually works best when you get sick at school. Start slow and let it build."

I listen as she gives me all the details. I almost take paper to write things down, but as if she can read my mind, she warns me.

"You're not writing this down, are you? Stop. No evidence."

I nod my head again and work hard to commit everything to memory.

It's going to be complicated and I have to plan every last detail. But it has to work.

That's all there is to it.

Chapter 46
Thursday

The Deed Is Done

I get to school with everything I need. No one sees me take anything from the fridge or put a concoction together. Not even Sarah the snoop. It's D Day and D time will begin before lunch.

I think back on my instructions. "Use the bathroom next to the cafeteria and throw the bag you used away in one of the lunch cans as you head to the nurse's office. No one will ever go through that gross trash."

Check.

"Miss the toilet just a little so if someone checks, there's some evidence."

Check.

"Use a mint afterward. That way, if they smell your breath, they'll think you used it because your mouth tasted gross. Normal breath is a dead giveaway that you're faking it."

Check.

I study my 'sick face' in the mirror for a minute. It looks

fake. Too sick. I don't want them calling an ambulance. If I think about how horrible I feel lying about everything, my face looks perfect.

At least my thoughts can be real.

On to the nurse's office.

It takes Mom ten minutes to get to school. It normally takes ten minutes to get Sarah in her car seat. Mom comes in by herself.

"Where are the little guys?" I say, sitting up on the cot as soon as she comes in, alone.

"Mrs. Roberts ran over to watch them. Jada was napping, so. . . ."

I haven't thought about the extra trouble I'm causing Mom. I feel my eyes fill with tears. "Sorry, Mom. I'm so sorry."

Mom kneels in front of me. "Don't worry about it, sweetie. You can't help getting sick. I'm sorry I didn't say anything this morning. I thought you looked off."

That's it. I break down and cry, loud sobs racking my chest, I tuck my head into her shoulder.

"I know how embarrassing it can be throwing up in school," she says, rubbing my back while I try to stop crying. "In fourth grade, I threw up all over the shoes of the boy I had a crush on. I'd been trying to present this perfect little girl image. It was the year we'd moved and I wanted friends, desperately. And there I was, spewing on the cutest boy in the class."

She giggles, and I do a little cry giggle that causes a snort to come out.

She pulls back and hands me some tissues. "Of course, this means no Parent's night tonight. Dad will be disappointed. Maybe you've got the family superpower of getting sick at the wrong moments."

I give a half-smile, blow my nose, and head home with Mom.

No one smells my breath, or takes my temperature, or double-checks the bathroom to see if I've really thrown up.

I am home free.

And it feels awful.

Chapter 47
Thursday, Home

Confronted

I sit cross-legged on my bed with all my pictures in front of me. Is there anything here that can work as a theme?

A quick knock on the door and Sarah runs into the room. "Pictures!" she shouts and jumps on the bed. "I want to play."

I gather the pictures in my hands before she can ruin them. "Careful," I say. "I don't want them messed up."

"I won't mess them up," Sarah says. "I like your pictures. I like to pretend I'm in them."

I stare at her. "What do you mean?"

"Sometimes I come in here and play with them." She jumps off the bed, opens the drawer to my nightstand, and pulls out another photo. "You missed one."

It's the one I took of the smushed dog poop at the park.

"It looks like play-doh. I like to pretend I'm drawing in it."

"It does kind of look like that," I say. "But, please don't get into my things again."

Sarah puts a finger to her lips, just like Mom sometimes

does, and says, "I'll think about it." Then she leaves the room.

"Close the door," I shout after her. I'll be asking Mom and Dad for a lock for my room.

Instead of closing the door, Sarah comes around the corner and says, "Phone for you."

I slip the pictures back in the drawer and run to the phone.

"You went home sick. Were you really?" Porter asks. His voice is louder and stronger than his usual, relaxed self.

"I, um," I say. I can't think of what I should say. Lying is becoming pretty easy, but with such a direct question my tongue gets all twisted.

"Marsha and I are coming over," he says. "We have to talk."

"But, I'm. . . ." Again, my tongue stops working. I try to change the subject. "The Parent's Night," I say.

"There's time. We won't stay long."

I wait for them on the front stoop. I brought the picture I took on the swing, Bly's blurry life. I'm not sure I'll show them. But when Porter said we have to talk, I thought about bringing this picture. Maybe, if I get brave, I can show them to help explain how I feel. I don't know if words will work as well as the picture.

Everything hurts. Not like a bruise or a stomachache, but like all the cells in my body are tired of lying. Tired of being on edge all the time in case something spills out. Tired of being afraid of someone finding out who I really am.

What do they want? What will I say? How much will I tell

them?

Porter pulls up on his bike before I've decided anything other than to listen to what he says, but my heart is beating out of my chest. Porter's not just the kind of smart that can remember the names of all the bones in your body by looking at a list for a minute. He's the kind who can put little facts together and figure out how they relate.

What if he knows my truth? What if he's here to say we can never again be friends because of how stupid I am?

Marsha runs up from the park moments later. She's out of breath, but the look on her face is one I've never seen before. She looks strong. Maybe even fierce. There isn't a bit of "Mousy Marsha" showing anywhere.

"Hey," Porter says, sitting on the top step next to me.

"Hey," I say.

Marsha stands a few steps down, holding onto the railing.

"We've been friends for five years, right?" he asks, looking straight ahead.

"Five years on Halloween," I say, rubbing my hands across my pants.

"Remember when I told you about the explosion in the basement, and you helped me figure out what to do?"

"The one that had spaghetti noodles hanging from the ceiling?" I can't help it. I laugh. And Porter laughs with me. It feels good, until his next sentence, then the tightness in all of my cells comes back, worse than before.

"So, why can't you trust me now?" He turns and stares at me. Then he nods to include Marsha. "Trust us."

155

I shift in my seat. "What do you mean?" I ask, looking across the street.

"Look at me, Blyster. Look right at me," he says, his voice raised and stern.

I glance quickly but turn away. Something about his eyes looks too real, too trusting. And I don't trust myself to not tell them everything.

What will happen if I do?

He puts a finger on my chin and turns my head so I'm facing him. I can see Marsha and now she has her arms crossed like Mom when she is about to lecture me.

"I know you, Bly. I've never seen you lie to your parents. And you called in sick today when you looked fine this morning and you admitted you hadn't told your parents about not being in Mathletes."

"I saw the look on your face when you hid something from Mrs. Brimhall," Marsha says. "And something was weird with you and Cherie at the park the other day. Things aren't adding up."

"Every time I see you, you look haunted," says Porter. "Like you're being chased by something you can't see." He picks up a pebble next to him and throws it down to the street. "Friends help each other. Let us help you."

That does it. I can't hold the story in anymore. I take the picture from my pocket and hold it flat in my hand for them to see. Marsha bends closer to see it. If they can understand this, maybe I'll tell them more. "This is my life," I say.

They both look at me like they are waiting for me to say

more. *Do I want to say more?* My chest hurts, like it's pushing words out from deep down inside of me. I open my mouth and let the words come. "It's blurry because that's how I feel. Like I'm so confused about things. But if I share those things, maybe it will get worse." I'm not feeling brave enough to say the next words, that they might not be my friends anymore.

Porter takes the picture and studies it, like the answers are all inside the blur. That's okay. I know he works things out by studying them first. But what will Marsha do? I don't have to wait long to find out. She sits next to me and gives me a giant hug.

"When my parents died, I felt just like that," she says, still hugging me.

And that undoes me. Like a spinning top that has been wound up and is let go. I have enough sense to check that no one else can hear, and then I spill it all. It comes out fast, and kind of jumbled. My grades, my cheating, my fears and hopes. And they take the whole thing in without running away screaming about how they'll never be my friend ever again.

When I finish, Marsha pulls an embroidered handkerchief from her pocket and hands it to me. I blow my nose and wipe my eyes.

"So, she assumed you'd cheat for her on the science report?" Marsha asks.

"Yes. And she was right, I did need her. I used her advice to know how to fake sick. Besides, she's so sure of herself, I don't think I'd know how to say no," I say, taking a deep breath.

I'm hoping my crying won't give me the hiccups. That'll

157

be a giveaway to Mom that I've been crying. I'm amazed she's let me stay out here so long, thinking I'm sick. She must be making dinner.

Porter shakes his head. Maybe it takes a while for him to register what I've done. Maybe now he'll tell me how we can't be friends anymore.

I can't stand not knowing.

"Porter?" I ask.

"You can't do this anymore, Bly. You know that, right?" Porter stands up and starts pacing.

"I don't want to, that's the thing. I wanted to, at first. I thought a little more time and I'd be able to bring my grades up and everything would be okay. I thought that as soon as my grades were okay, I could get brave and tell Dad I want to be in photography club instead of Mathletes. But it's been almost two weeks and my grades haven't gone up one bit. In fact, they've gone down in gym and sewing. Who fails gym and sewing?" I ask, worked up now and pacing along with Porter.

Marsha holds out her hands and says, "Stop." She stands in front of Porter and me. "We need to come up with a plan, just like you guys did when Porter destroyed the basement. We can do this, Bly."

I have to ask the question. Otherwise, it'll sit in my brain and drill holes where birds will build nests and I'll be even dumber than I am now. "So. . . . will you guys still be my friends, now that you know how stupid I am?"

Marsha grabs my hand and smiles. "Of course," she says. "I would be the stupid one if I ended our friendship. Who else will turn my hair into a Zen garden?"

Porter's mouth drops open. He gives Marsha a weird look and she shrugs. He shakes his head like he's trying to let go of that image. Then he looks like a fish breathing with his mouth for a few seconds before he starts talking. "What do you think, Blyster? Looks like not only do you not have faith in yourself or your parents, but you don't have faith in me. Don't ask me that again." He sits, and motions for me to sit next to him. "Now, we've got five minutes to come up with a plan to end this, then I've got to get home."

It only takes three.

Chapter 48
Friday, After School

The Plan Begins

Cherie leans against the locker next to me and studies her fingernails. "So, how's the actress?"

I fumble in my locker, searching for my math notebook. "What do you mean?" I ask. Being near her makes me squirm.

"Feeling better?" she asks.

"Oh, that. Yeah." Then I remember my plan with Porter. I turn to her, paying more attention. "Thanks."

"You know you'll need me again, right?" She asks, still not looking me in the eye. "We've got a good thing going. Like my Daddy does at work. He calls it, "You scratch my back, I scratch yours."

"Sounds like you've got something in mind," I say, my stomach churning.

She nods and looks around, probably looking for anyone who might overhear things. "Monday's test in Geography. You've got it two periods before me. He says there'll be two essay questions, one paragraph each. That's all I need."

"But how am I supposed to get the answers to you? They'll be on my test paper that I turned in." I ask.

"Look, we're gonna miss the bus. I'll call you with details." Cherie walks off as pretty and sweet looking as can be.

I stand for a minute watching her. How different her reality is from the front she puts up. But aren't I doing the same thing? I turn around and look in my locker, still not finding my math notebook.

Some kids run down the hall, one yelling, "Hold the bus!"

"Bus!!" I yell, slamming my locker, grabbing my backpack, and running as fast as I can to the bus area.

It isn't fast enough.

Chapter 49
Monday, D Day

There is a Fire Alright—a Backfire

Porter and I spend an hour on the phone Sunday working out details of our plan. I call Marsha when we're done to let her know her part. If the plan doesn't work, it'll go down in flames with me at the bottom. Porter has my camera and I feel weird not having it with me. I've brought the envelope I'll need and the rest is a matter of timing.

The handoff will take place right after geography in the art hallway by the water fountain. Marsha will cue me when Cherie makes it to the corner of the hall. It might make me late for math, but I have to chance it. Porter will get an excuse to leave his class early, but it's his favorite teacher, so he knows it'll work.

I wander down the art hallway, smelling the fumes. One room smells like paint and another like glue, the yucky smelling kind. I see Porter's shoe sticking out from behind a row of lockers, right where he should be.

Marsha gives a thumbs up and I know I need to be ready.

Cherie comes around the corner, her usual, confident self. I walk towards her, pacing myself to get in front of Porter at the same time she does. It's hard not to look at him. That'll give away everything. So I keep my eyes on a spot behind Cherie on the other side of the hallway than Porter. Five more steps. . . four. . . three. . . two. . . one. . . pass the envelope.

Click. . . whirr. I hope he's aimed right.

Cherie turns on her heels and faces the sound. It doesn't take her long to figure out what's going on. She lunges at Porter, but he holds the camera and the developing photo above his head. Even jumping, she can't get close. In trying to reach the picture, she drops the envelope and it slides across the floor. I grab it a second before she gets there and stuff it down my tucked-in shirt.

And that's when things get ugly.

"Grrrr," Cherie's guttural sound is scarier than her fist coming at my face. That's probably why I don't duck.

I've never been punched before. Hearing the punch on my jaw from both the outside and the inside echo would have been an amazing thing to think about, except that I have to put more thought into not slamming my head against the lockers.

Instead, my shoulder slams into a locker, tearing my shirt and hurting so bad all I want to do is to hurt back. I run at her, knocking her to the ground. The past weeks of fear and anger and self-loathing all come out in fury towards Cherie as I sit on her stomach and try to hit her wherever I can. But she's fast and grabs my arms before I can land more than one punch on her pretty pouty mouth. She pushes me and grabs my ponytail, pulling me off her. We both stand but I'm off balance with her twisting my hair around.

I hear noises in the background. We must be attracting a crowd, but most of the noise is probably my screaming as she continues to pull my hair. I twist fast and I grab her leg, pulling her off-balance, and we're both scrambling on the floor. Just as she rips my shirt the rest of the way open and grabs the envelope, a large, brown hand comes down in between us and takes it from her. Arms come from somewhere and pull us apart, both of us shaking and panting.

The look of hatred on Cherie's face has almost as much power as her first punch.

I collapse on the ground, holding my shirt closed, and break down in sobs.

This isn't part of the plan.

Chapter 50
Monday, Mr. Kamai's Office

It All Spills Out

Porter walks out of Mr. Kamai's office, giving me a small smile, and ignoring Cherie. At least we have evidence and it's in the hands of Mr. Kamai. And Porter is the kind of kid every teacher and leader respects and listens to. I was as well, before this year. Marsha was far enough away that she doesn't get caught and Porter said last night that if we went to show the evidence, he'd leave her out of it. It's better that way.

The secretary loans me some old sweatshirt from the lost and found to put over my torn shirt. As warm as it should be, I'm shivering. I can hear Cherie breathing hard next to me and I'm glad grownups are around in case she attacks me again.

This is my second visit to the vice principal's office in two weeks. The second visit in my entire life.

How did I think I could figure this out by myself?

Porter and Marsha convinced me that this is what we need to do. They promised me they don't care what kinds of grades I get. We're friends and friends stick together. I wish they could be with me through this part, but I guess there're some things we have to do by ourselves. But Porter is sure my parents can handle knowing the truth. Not only that, he promised they'll help me. I cling to his words as I wait for everything to be sorted out.

The door opens and Mr. Kamai steps out. "Shall I talk to you both together or one at a time?"

My mouth opens, but no words come out.

Cherie doesn't have that problem. "Doesn't matter. Just know that she'll lie, no matter what. She doesn't know how to tell the truth." She looks down at her nails, fingering one that was chipped, maybe from our fight.

I shrug my shoulders. If I try to talk, I know I'll burst into tears and that'll be even more embarrassing.

"Then, I'll talk to Blythe first, and you can straighten me out. Blythe?"

He motions with his fingers and I do my best to stand and walk. I'm shaking so bad, I think maybe I'll just wobble a step or two and then fall, but somehow I make it a few steps, holding onto the door frame to catch my breath before I take the next steps to the seat he's pulled out for me.

I sit, hugging my backpack, my head down, studying the corner of his desk calendar.

He sits too, and things are quiet for a minute.

I concentrate on slowing my breathing, still keeping my head down. If I see his face, I know it'll be too much to handle.

"Your friend, Porter vouched for you. He said Cherie started the fight. I believe him." Mr. Kamai's hands stretch out

166

partway across his desk and I see his knuckles and a wedding ring.

I raise my eyes enough to see his thumbs pushed together, but that's as high as I can go.

"Of course, that doesn't mean you should have fought back."

I drop my eyes back to his knuckles and squeak, "No."

"Does that mean, 'no, I shouldn't have fought back,' or 'no, I should have fought back?" He laughs. It's a rich laugh and warms some of the shivering out of me.

I take a deep breath and raise my eyes up to a button on the front of his shirt. "I shouldn't have fought back."

"Good answer. Now, about this plan of yours and this. . . information sharing." He holds the unopened envelope in front of him, dangling it low enough that I can see it.

Does he mean the information Porter shared with him? The picture of Cherie taking the envelope from me? Or does he mean how Cherie and I have been, well, sharing information for the last few weeks? I guess they're connected enough that it doesn't really matter.

"I don't want to open it just yet. Porter gave me some idea of why you may have done what you did. Not the best excuse I've heard."

My head lowers back down to his hands.

"Young lady. I've seen enough of the top of your head. While a fine head, I'd like to see your face. I don't bite."

I hear Porter's voice in my head, 'You can do this, Blyster. I don't care about your grades. You're my friend.' And I see

167

Marsha smiling her biggest smile when I gave her the picture of her hair. I hold onto the promise that they'll still be my friends. With another deep breath, I lift my head and look eye to eye with Mr. Kamai.

"I cheated by helping Cherie. And she signed a progress report for me. And paid me. And showed me how to fake sick. I wanted to get my grades up before my parents found out. I thought if I tried harder, I could get my grades up and no one would know. It was wrong. Then I felt stuck in it. I wasn't brave enough to pull myself out."

"But you were brave enough. And you did," Mr. Kamai says. "While I don't applaud what you did or how you tried to solve it, I do applaud that you had the guts to do so. Now, do you have any idea why Cherie wanted your help?"

"No," I say, thinking. "I mean, she seems smart." I think again and remember something. "Wait. Maybe. Hang on." Tearing through my backpack, I hope the paper will still be there. Throwing loose papers and notebooks onto Mr. Kamai's desk, I search through everything. I see a small crumpled paper in the bottom corner of my bag. I pull it out and hand it to him. "This. It's from Cherie."

He takes the paper and uncrumples it. " 'I clal u.' That doesn't make sense. What are you saying?"

"Cherie wrote it to me. She meant 'I'll call you.' And she never wanted to write anything in science class. At first, I thought she was being lazy, but I'm wondering. . . ."

"If she is having trouble writing. Hmm. We'll have to see. Let's bring her in here and open this envelope up in front of both of you." He motions to the junk I'd left on his desk. "Put this stuff away, please."

As Mr. Kamai goes to the door to ask Cherie in, I clean my things off his desk.

Chapter 51
Monday, The Drive Home

Silence

Dad picks me up.

Chapter 52
Monday, Night

At the Bottom of the Fire

Didn't I say that our family doesn't go to the principal's office? Our family knows how to behave in school." Dad paces the same spot as last time. Up and down. I can almost feel the carpet fibers begging for mercy.

But I'm the one who needs to beg for mercy.

"I'm sorry, I'm sorry, I'm sorry," I wail.

"We don't need sorrys," Dad says. "We need to know what's going on." He has that look that always scares me. Not that he'll hurt me, or anything like that. His being disappointed in me is worse than some kind of spanking or grounding.

I drop down near the door, too ashamed to get closer. "Seventh grade is too hard. I can't do it anymore."

Right then, Sarah walks into the room, flying one of her ponies around. "My pony is in seventh grade and he likes it." She dives the pony around Dad's legs. He picks Sarah up and flies her out of the room, Superman-style.

Part of me hopes he won't come back for a while. As hard

as it is to talk about it with Mom, it's even harder when Dad is there. His bragging to people about how smart I am, telling them I'm going to take over their jobs someday, was fun when I was little, but not so much anymore. Instead, it makes me feel like a big disappointment.

"Bly?"

I look up. Mom comes down to me, her feet tucked under her, her hand under my chin. Her face is blurred. I wipe my eyes and sniff. She hands me a wadded-up tissue from her pocket. "It's clean," she says.

I take it, give a blow, and put it in my own jeans pocket.

Mom presses her forehead against mine and wraps her arms around my shoulders. "I know this person," she begins. "It's not me, I swear. She, I mean this person, is having a hard time at school and is afraid to tell his/her parents. Any suggestions as to how we can help this person?"

I give a little giggle, despite myself. Then I take a deep breath and let it out slowly. "I don't know what's wrong. Everything is so hard. And the teachers don't like me this year, and. . . ." I see Dad walk in out of the corner of my eye. His hard face stops me in the middle of my sentence.

"How many people are you going to find to blame this on, Bly? You've blamed the teachers. How else can we spread this out and make it so it's not your fault?" Dad drops down hard on the chair next to us. He puts his head into his hands and rubs his hands around in circles, giving his face monster shapes.

This is something he does when he doesn't know what to do. The last time I saw it was when we found out Jada was

172

going to be born too early and there was nothing he could do about it. Putting his clothing into the closet in color order or making the perfect family chart would do nothing to stop nature.

None of my stall tactics seems like the best plan right now so I stay quiet.

So do Mom and Dad.

As I sit there in silence, my clothes seem to get tighter and tighter and the room warmer and warmer. I have to say something before my clothes squeeze the life out of me.

We sit there so long, it seems as if it must be the next morning already, but I can still see the sun sinking through the blinds opposite me. I can't stand it any longer, so I stand up and shout, "I try and I try and I try. I'm just stupid. That's all there is to it."

I run out of the room, hoping no one will follow me. Sometimes I act like I don't want to be followed, but I really do. Right now, I for sure don't. There's nothing to say but that I'm stupid and a cheater and don't try hard enough and I'm a loser and don't deserve anything, let alone entering a photography contest or having friends or anything.

When I get to my room I don't slam my door, even though I really want to. That might bring one of my parents up; door slamming is a definite no at our house. Closing it as gently as I can force myself, I turn around to find Sarah sitting on my bed.

"I heard you tell Mommy you were stupid," she says, combing the hair on her pretty pony. "But I know you're not.

Remember those cool pictures we played with? They're smart."

I open my mouth to deny it, but I close it before any words come out. When I was with Marsha and Porter, Marsha understood my feelings just by looking at a picture I took. That showed her smartness, but it also showed mine. I was able to use a picture I took to show a feeling. And that must be some kind of smart. It's something I'll need to think about. But right now all I want to think about is how miserable I am. I kneel down by the bed and put my arms around her. "Thanks, Sarah. I need to be by myself now, okay?"

"Okay," she says and she jumps down and flies her pony out of the room.

I fall forward onto the bed and pull myself up from the floor. My whole body feels itchy, even my brain. Here I am, trying to figure things out, be a good student and please my parents and it all blows up in my face.

Is it even worth it?

I don't know anymore.

Deciding a shower might wash off some of the itchies, I roll off the bed, grab my robe and slip into the bathroom for a long, hot shower.

*****

I've gone to bed in my robe, hair still wrapped in the towel. There's a soft tapping on the door. Answering means I have to open my mouth and that's too much work. The door squeaks and a line of light crosses my face.

"Are you awake?" Mom's voice is soft, tentative. I hear her tiptoe across my floor, crackling some papers. The bed creaks and moves me a little as she sits down.

I peek one eye open, roll to the side, and give a short grunt.

"I know you're too upset to talk about this now, but we'll need to talk soon. If you're truly trying, we need to figure out what's going on. If you're not, we need to figure that out, too. We're proud of you for being brave enough to end things with Cherie. And in quite a dramatic fashion. Maybe you should join Drama Club instead of Mathletes." She giggles.

I'm too exhausted to attempt a smile.

"For now, get a good night's sleep. We love you." She kisses my cheek and I feel her lift herself from my bed.

I know I have to say something and I work up the energy for a short sentence. "Mom, I'm sorry."

Mom sits back down. She rubs my back and says, "I need to know. Why didn't you say something sooner?"

I take a deep breath and decide I can tell a little bit. Maybe telling will make me less tired. I'll have fewer secrets to carry around. "Dad always calls me his little professor," I say. I grab a tissue off my nightstand and wipe my eyes. "It makes me feel like I have to always be smart."

With the moonlight coming through the window, I see Mom's head bob up and down.

"I see," she says. "Have you told him that? You can always talk to Dad or me, about anything. Our job is to listen and help you sort things out. Sometimes it takes Dad a few minutes to settle into something, but you know he's kind and fair."

I push up on my elbows and look at Mom's profile. Half

of it is in the light and half in the dark. It would a great picture. Instead of grabbing my camera, I say the next big thing. "He might. . . think less of me if he knows I'm not smart."

There is silence. I don't know if it's a good silence or a bad silence. My itching comes back again.

When she talks, it's soft and slow. "You know Jada was born early?"

"Yeah?"

"We haven't said much about it, and it's a little early to know for sure. But the doctor thinks because of her difficult start, she might have some learning challenges."

I nod my head. "Like how I thought she should be crawling and you said we need to give her more time. And then she crawled on her first birthday and we all cheered."

"Yeah, that's an example." Mom reaches for my hand and puts it on her cheek. Her skin is smooth and cool. "Do you think we love Jada any less because it took her longer to crawl, or because she isn't walking yet?"

Tears pour down my cheeks. I shake my head. I know how much we all love Jada, and that love won't change if something about her changes. So, maybe that means Dad's love won't change, even if something about me changes.

I take a deep breath, but it wobbles a little with the tears, and I shake my head again. I don't have any words.

She leans down and gives me a hug. "Things will be okay, my sweet girl. We will always love you. We'll figure this out more tomorrow. Okay?"

I nod my head.

"Good night."

The door closes and I lay in the dark thinking. Is this really going to work out? Mom makes it sound simple. But it isn't simple. Part of me feels better about some things, but I'm suspended for the rest of the week and then have only two days of school to get my grades up enough to join photography club and enter the contest.

Things aren't simple at all.

Chapter 53
Tuesday

Picture Perfect?

You'll need to watch the kids while I gather your school-work," Mom says, grabbing her purse and jacket from the closet. "Jada should nap a little longer. Mason's bus will be here in about five minutes. Snack is on the counter." Mom steps out the door, closing it tightly behind her.

I lumber down the stairs, still in my pajamas, my hair uncombed. Normally, I'd have enjoyed a day off like this, reading, or rereading a favorite book. But I can't concentrate on anything. I want my homework. It's the only way I'll have a chance of bringing my grades up and entering the contest.

If my parents will let me enter. We haven't finished our 'discussion' on my behavior. I know I don't deserve anything but punishment for what I've done. And, I've known it's coming since Porter, Marsha, and I came up with our plan.

But that doesn't make it easier.

Sarah comes into the kitchen with something in her hands and starts laying it out on the table.

My photos!

"Sarah! I told you to leave those alone!"

"But I like them," she says, moving them around on the table like puzzle pieces.

I sigh and sit down with her. "Okay, fine. Let's play a game. We have eighteen pictures here. Pick out a group of six that fit together."

"Fit together?" she asks. "Like a puzzle?"

"No." I think about how I can explain theme to a four-year-old. "Like, our family. We're all different, but we go together."

I like that thought. I'd decided that I must not fit in this family because I'm not smart like everyone thinks I am. But maybe that doesn't matter. Mom made me feel like I might still fit. Maybe it's possible I fit in a different way than I thought. My head spins with the idea.

Sarah moves pictures around the table, grouping them different ways, like the classification system.

"Careful," I say. "Keep your fingers on the white part only or you'll mess them up."

Sarah shifts her fingers back. "Okay. I like this one best," She says, pointing to one of my first attempts.

"But why? That's my thumb in the corner. It's a mistake."

"Why does that make it a mistake? That's why I like it," Sarah says, turning to give me a hug. "You're in it. That makes it the best."

I hug her back. "Sarah, how do you always know what to say?"

"I don't know," she says, shrugging her tiny shoulders. "Maybe I'm smart like you."

That deserves a second hug.

Chapter 54
Tuesday Night

The Hard and the Soft

Dad, stop staring at me," I say, looking up from my geography homework.

"Then start doing your homework instead of gazing into space for ten minutes," Dad says. He sits across from me at the kitchen table, a book open in front of him.

We finished discussing my cheating and my biggest punishment will be homework time with Dad every night. . . along with being grounded for two weeks. It still feels like Dad cares more about my grades than he does about me.

I stare at my geography again, but my mind whirls. I have to try harder. I stare harder. It doesn't work. I stand, knocking my chair over. "Crumb bum! Can I please do a gym assignment? Then I'll come back to this." I pick up the chair before Dad can yell at me.

"Fine," Dad says with a harrumph. "Go for a walk with Sarah, You'll both need jackets. Take my phone so you have a timer."

The weather is chilly, so I keep my hands in my pockets instead of holding hands with Sarah. I've brought my backpack with Polly in her special pocket. You never know when a good picture will show up.

Sarah hops around me as I walk towards the park.

"Watch out, I'm going to trip over you," I say as I stop short to avoid a fall.

"Take a picture of me skipping," Sarah says, now hopping in place.

I pull my camera out. Most of my pictures so far have been close-ups of things I found interesting. Things people might have fun at guessing what they are. But Sarah gave me an idea when we played with the photos on the table. Her favorite is the one with my thumb in the corner. I thought it ruined the whole thing, but she thought it made it the best.

What if I take some pictures of mistakes that aren't bad?

Sarah's version of skipping can be the first.

"Okay. Let's wait until we get to the park and find a good spot," I say. "Come on. Race you!"

The photo is just right.

*****

Getting ready for bed, I rethink what Sarah said earlier. She wondered why my thumb in a picture made it a mistake. My first thought is that of course it's a mistake, I didn't mean to have it there and it messes up the whole picture. Sitting on my bed, I pull the picture out of my drawer and look again.

I remember Mom telling me that the first time someone made my favorite cookie, chocolate chip, it was a mistake. And

Mr. Bines said that the guy who invented penicillin found it because of a mistake. He said penicillin has saved a bunch of lives.

So, are mistakes good? Maybe sometimes they are. And maybe sometimes they make the world better somehow. I can't see how my cheating made the world better, but I guess that wasn't really a mistake, it was more of a bad choice.

Forgetting homework is a mistake, because I don't do it on purpose. I'm not sure it makes the world a better place, but maybe thinking about it and working on it. . . maybe that makes me a better person.

The thought makes my brain spin a little and I know I'll have to think about it more. Maybe when I'm not so tired.

I slide the picture back in my drawer and decide I'll think about it later.

Chapter 55
Tuesday Night

Good and Bad Secrets

As I turn out my bedroom light and snuggle under the covers, I hear a knock at my door.

"Come in," I say.

A sliver of light hits my face and then darkens around the shape of my dad. He closes the door behind him and tiptoes to my bed. "May I sit?" he asks.

"Sure," I say, moving over to make room for him.

The bed bends with his weight and I roll into him. His arm goes around me and he kisses my cheek.

"I've been hard on you," he says.

"I," I start, but he cuts me off.

"Wait, let me say what I need to. Then I'll listen to you. I've been thinking and I'm afraid if I wait, it'll get harder to say."

With the light shining in a gap in the window shade from a streetlight, I can see his outline in profile. I have his nose, a bit large and strong, going straight all the way down. Some of his hair curls up at the ends, by his ears. He usually gets a haircut before that happens. His head is downcast, his eyelids blinking. Looking at him this way, my strong, know-it-all father looks vulnerable. It's not something I'm used to seeing.

I nod.

"I've been hard on you. I've expected perfection; in the same way my parents expected it from me. It made me work hard, harder than I would have otherwise, I think, and I've wanted that for you. I saw from when you were a toddler that you are exceptional. Now, all parents think their kids are exceptional." He gives a small laugh. "And they are, in their own ways. But I can tell that your mind is incredible and I began to dream about what you could be, what you would invent, or what medical cure you'd come up with, and I liked those thoughts. They made me feel that my small world as a humble professor was worthwhile because my daughter was going to save lives." He shifts and runs his hand through my hair. "I've been trying to live my life through you. Not giving you a chance to find your own way. That's not fair of me."

He pauses.

I let the words sink in. They're kind of heavy, like I'll have to keep thinking about what they mean for a long time. But at the same time, they make a certain part of me want to float in the air; relieved of a terrible burden I didn't know I was carrying.

I sniff, not realizing I've been crying. He pulls tissues from the box on my nightstand, gives one to me, and blows his nose with the other one.

"Now, this doesn't mean that your behavior is acceptable. Not at all," he continues. "But it does mean that I realize that perhaps the pressure I put on you to be who you weren't may have added to the problem."

I sit up and put my arms around him, burying my head against his shoulder long enough for the moisture of my tears on his shirt to get cold. His head rests on top of mine and his arms hold me, making me feel as safe as I had as a little girl, before my worries of being good enough began to dominate my life.

"Thank you, Daddy," I say, the words squeaking out an octave higher than normal.

"Have you really been trying hard to succeed in school this year?" Dad asks.

I know the answer, but decide to think it over before I say anything. He's admitted some things about himself that must have been really hard to say. It deserves me making sure I'm being just as open. And that means thinking before I answer. I consider all the times I caught myself not paying attention and then tried again, the times I went to get homework and books out of my locker and then something caught my eye and I forgot, and the many times I did homework, working really hard on it, and left it at home.

"I have," I say, wiping my nose on the tissue again. "Something about this year is different. It's like everything is a thousand times harder. When I started cheating, I thought if I just did it for a few things, I'd be able to get caught up. But it never seemed to help. I know it wasn't the right thing to do, but I felt like I was stuck in a deep hole and cheating was the only rope I could see."

"The most important rope I want you to always remember is your parents. That rope will constantly be there. I'm much more disappointed in your choices than I ever could be about your grades." He strokes the side of my face and it feels like the truth of his words flows through his fingers and into my head.

I manage a small smile, though in the dark, I'm not sure he can see it.

"Let's make a promise to each other," he said. "You promise to always be honest with us, and I'll promise to always hear you out, and think before I react."

"What about Christmas secrets and other surprises?" I ask. I know he doesn't mean to include them, but I need a moment to ponder. Is this a promise I can keep? Tanner family promises are unbreakable. It's like a law or something. I'm usually pretty honest, but what if I have a really good reason to lie?

The moment I think the word lie, I get that old sick feeling in my stomach again, and I know what I need to do.

"Christmas secrets and other surprises don't count," he says. "Ready?"

I nod.

And then we do it, our Tanner Family Pact Shake*.

He kisses my forehead and lays me back down, tucking the covers up to my chin.

"Now," he says, in more of a playful mood, "what's this I

hear from Sarah about you being an awesome photographer?"
He smiles.

*I can't tell what it is. It's a good kind of secret.

Chapter 56
Wednesday, School Meeting

Surrounded by Grownups

Walking into school with my parents for a parent/ teacher/student meeting has me shaking all over. I concentrate on the file folder in my hand, filled with the overdue assignments I've completed. Without Dad sitting next to me and helping me put things in the right places, the folder wouldn't have been nearly as thick.

As we get to the conference room, the door opens and Cherie walks out with her parents. Her mom looks grim, but her dad looks as though he's going to punch someone. Cherie's head is down, her walk far from her normal confident bounce. She puts a hand up to scratch her face and I notice that her nails are chipped and ragged.

The room is filled with grownups—mostly my teachers, but also Ms. Bowers and Mr. Kamai. They sit in comfy-looking chairs around a table larger than my grandma's table at Thanksgiving. I sit between Mom and Dad, and immediately lean back and almost fall over backward. I guess the chairs aren't meant for leaning back.

My teachers are a mixed bunch. Ms. Carter is scowling. Her scowl, along with her black dress, makes me think of a witch. Mr. Scott looks serious, but his eyes are soft and when he catches my eye he winks. The rest are a blur as I try to focus on breathing without throwing up. Mom and Dad both squeeze my hands. I wonder if they're as nervous as I am.

Ms. Bowers speaks first. "As you all know, we're here to discuss Miss Tanner's schoolwork and struggles, focusing on what we can do to assist her to succeed."

That doesn't sound too bad.

Ms. Carter speaks first. "I know what she can do. She can start working harder and focusing on her studies instead of constantly playing around."

She barely has a chance to finish before Mr. Scott speaks up. "Sometimes it isn't a matter of working harder but a matter of finding what works for you and then working smarter."

Ms. Carter harrumphs.

"If you don't mind, Ms. Bowers," Mr. Scott continues, "I'd like to tell you about what I've noticed with Bly and make a suggestion. It's nothing we'll be able to come to a conclusion with at this point, but it may send us the right direction." He winks at me again, making the rock in my stomach a bit lighter.

"Go ahead, Mr. Scott," Ms. Bowers says. "You've been very helpful already. Perhaps you ought to think of becoming a school counselor with your observation skills."

There's a smattering of laughter around the table, though Ms. Carter remains still, her dry lips begging for lip balm. I'd hand her mine if I didn't think her glare would fry me in my seat.

Mr. Scott speaks again. "I've been watching Bly and have seen from the beginning of the year that she is bright, willing, and working hard to achieve."

Dad squeezes my hand. For the first time since we've been in the room, I'm sure there's a teacher on my side.

Mr. Scott continues. "I've also noticed that she's often somewhere else in her mind during class, struggles to stay on task, and doesn't bring in most of her assignments on time."

Maybe I thought too soon. Maybe he isn't on my side. The rock in my stomach comes back, heavier than ever. Mom squeezes my other hand.

"I have the suspicion," Mr. Scott says, "that Bly may be dealing with something like ADHD. Her natural intelligence and general desire to please may have carried her this far in school without it being picked up on. And, now, perhaps, she's hit a wall."

Some of the teachers, including Mr. Bines, turn to each other and murmur some things. I see a head or two nod.

Coach Peabody speaks up. "The kids I've known with ADHD have excelled in gym class. That's not the case with her."

I want to yell and say, "I'm in the room! Don't talk about me like I'm not here." It didn't bother me when Mr. Scott did it because he'd look at me sometimes, including me in the conversation.

Then I think maybe Coach Peabody has a point. Who fails gym class?

Mr. Scott speaks again. "Often kids with ADHD have the hyperactive kind, and those kids normally do excel when movement is involved. And their school struggles are often picked up when they're very young. But there's another kind that is quieter, without the hyperactivity, and can be missed easily." Mr. Scott sighs and looks at my parents. "I'm not a doctor. Nothing like it. But I know kids. I think it's worth you taking her to the doctor to be evaluated."

My parents look at each other and my dad shrugs. I don't know whether to be happy that maybe my problem has a name, or to be upset that there's something wrong with me, but my face feels hot at being talked about for so long.

Ms. Bowers speaks next. "Does anyone else have something to add?" No one speaks for what feels like forever.

I feel Dad shift in his seat. Then he speaks. "We'll make a doctor's appointment for her right away. I've heard a bit about ADHD. Is this inherited?"

Ms. Bowers answers. "The jury's still out on causes, but it's thought that inheritance is a possibility. I don't think there's much more we can do until Bly is evaluated by her physician. At that point, we can reconvene, in part or in whole, to discuss how to proceed." She looks at me. "I'm sure this has been awkward for you, Ms. Tanner, to be surrounded by and talked about by adults. Thank you for putting up with us. Do you have anything you'd like to add?"

I feel my face turning shades of red, probably even purple, as all eyes turn to me. I think for a moment, swallow hard, and stand. "I'm sorry for the," I swallow hard again, trying to get the lump in my throat to go down, "the things I've done to try and cover my. . . problem. . . . And I promise not to cheat again. Ever. It isn't worth it." I push the file folder forward and sit as fast as I can. Mom and Dad are right there for a hug so I can bury my head and not see anyone's reaction.

Surrounded by my parent's arms, I hear papers shuffling, chairs rolling and people whispering as they leave the room. Someone, probably Mr. Scott, rubs my head as he passes.

I hear Ms. Carter clear her throat. "I'm sorry for your recent loss," she says. I peek over my mom's shoulder and see Ms. Carter step out of the room. I stay, tucked away safely in my parents' arms until the room grows quiet.

"What was that about?" Mom asks.

Do I tell them? I take a big breath. May as well come clean and keep the Tanner Pact. "One of my homework excuses was attending a funeral for Lester."

Dad pulls me back to look in my eyes. "She's sorry our pet lizard died? She doesn't sound like the soft-hearted type, from either your description or this meeting."

I drop my eyes to the ground. "Somehow she got the impression he was my stepbrother." I look up at Dad with a little bit of pleading in my eyes, but I can't help but give a smirk as well.

Dad opens his mouth like he is going to start a lecture, but Mom giggles. "Let's call it quick thinking and move forward from here."

Dad smiles and the three of us leave quietly, but the silence feels like a warm bath and I almost smile.

Chapter 57
Friday

Doc, Yep, Looks Like ADHD

1) Papers about me to teachers and back again. Check.

2) Papers about me to parents and back again. Check.

3) Fill out questionnaire on my own behaviors. Doc said it should take fifteen minutes, but I get distracted by some kids in the waiting room playing with the trains. Check.

4) Nice (ha!) talk with doctor. Check.

5) Parent's nice (ha!) talk with the doctor. Check.

6) Doctor watching me interact with his setup. Check.

7) Prescription for some kind of medicine and explanation I'm too bored to listen to. Check.

8) Trying the medicine on a Saturday, not being hungry but cleaning my room like a madman. Check.

9) Being ungrounded for the weekend to see how the medicine changes things. Check.

10) Feeling like a science experiment but sometimes having the ability to think a thought all the way through. Priceless.

Chapter 58
Saturday

We Are > the Sum of Our Parts

With all my schoolwork done, at least what I'm allowed to turn in late, I spend Saturday working on my pictures for the contest. I have to have a 2.0 grade point average and I'm not sure if I'll make it, but I'm hopeful.

I love the idea Sarah gave me about the picture with my thumb on it and decide to run with that. With only ten pictures left in my roll, I have to be careful. Not much room for mistakes.

"Porter," I say, calling him on the phone. "Can you come over for a little bit? We can meet at the park."

"Sure," he says. "What for?"

"Oh, just to hang out," I say. I don't tell him I want to take his picture. If I did he might wear clothes that fit him better than his usual. And that is the imperfect part I want to get.

He looks his normal imperfect self.

"Stand on the swing," I say.

"Why?" He asks, stepping up without waiting for my explanation.

"Trust me," I say, pulling Polly out of my backpack.

He begins swinging, pushing forward with his feet, his sneakers ripped and untied, white socks showing several inches below too short jeans. "You're taking my picture? You want me to smile or be serious?" he says, slowing his swing.

"Um, eyes closed. Weird I know, but trust me. And stop for a minute so you're in focus." He doesn't need to know the picture will be of his feet. That'll be the fun surprise when we watch it develop.

He stills and the sun filters through the trees with a cool pattern right across his sock. Perfect!

Later that day I get a picture of Mom cleaning up a spill from the cookies she's baking and one of Mason taking apart a broken clock. Then one of Dad color-coding the calendar.

And only one mess up, where I grab Polly wrong and get a picture of my shoe. It's too imperfect to work.

I have five pictures now of cool but imperfect things and need one more. That one needs to be of me. The real me. Nothing fake. But how am I supposed to capture it? It doesn't work like a phone where you can see yourself if you flip the view. Since I have to take it myself to qualify, no cheating, I have to be careful about the setup. No wasting pictures. It takes a little thought, but then it comes to me.

"Sarah, come help me, please," I call down the hall after things are set up.

Sarah pitter-patters up the stairs. When she sees my camera, her face lights up. "I can help you take a picture?" she asks.

"Well, yes and no," I say. "The picture has to be taken by me for it to count for the contest. But I want you to look through this little window and tell me what you see. When I've turned it so you see me and my books, then I can press the button."

"Can I hold the picture when it comes out?"

"Sure," I say, glancing to check that her hands are clean.

I sit on the floor against my unmade bed, my math book leaning against me and my Sudoku book in my hand. I want to pretend to be working on it, but I have to hold the pencil and book in the same hand, so the other is free for the camera.

"Okay, Sarah. What do you see?"

She squints her eyes and looks. "My favorite sister in the whole wide world."

I keep my smile away just long enough to take the picture. Then we watch it develop together.

Chapter 59
Tuesday, School

A New and Improved??

My first day back after being suspended, I feel as though everyone's staring at me. The versions of our story I hear:

> 1) Cherie and Bly fought and Cherie ended up in the hospital with a broken nose.
>
> 2) Cherie and Bly fought and Bly ended up in the hospital with a broken arm.
>
> 3) Cherie and some kid fought and all the cheerleaders helped Cherie and the kid died.
>
> 4) Bly punched out Cherie because she was holding hands with Porter. Poor Porter.

Taking the medicine makes my day feel kind of different. It mostly feels like things are more interesting and important, but it also kind of feels like I've left a part of me, the part that sees everything, at home in bed. And I don't want my lunch. Mom planned for that and packed some things that won't spoil so I can eat them later if I get hungry. I can't see Ms. Carter putting up with me eating in class, though.

Early to math, and still carrying my poster board with the photo entry, I glance around. I'm the first one in the room, besides the teacher. Ms. Carter has written a problem on the board.

18 +2x > 82

"More than thirty-two," I say.

"Excuse me?" Ms. Carter turns and stares at me.

"The answer," I say, pointing to the board.

"I haven't taught this concept yet, Ms. Tanner." Ms. Carter's eyes bore into me.

"Oh," I say. "Am I wrong? Cause, the way I figure it, if you want to get X alone, you just subtract the eighteen from the eighty-two, then divide by two."

Ms. Carter blinks.

Deciding to let her stew in my brilliance, I turn to go to my seat. Other people come in and there's a dull hum of voices, footsteps, and scraping chairs.

"Blythe?"

Turning back to Ms. Carter, I decide to go on the offensive. "You know, Ms. Carter, I'm not doing too well in your class, but I'm good at math. I just," I pause, thinking how much I want to say, especially since the room is filling up with other kids. When Marsha comes through the door and sees me, I notice her eyes get big, like she's worried for me. But I plow on with what I need to say. "I'm not very good at remembering homework sometimes. And, well, other things, but never mind about that." I take a deep breath and support my weight on her desk, knowing now it's her turn to shoot me down.

She might think I'm talking back enough to send me to the principal's office. Somehow, I don't care. I've had a month of hearing her remarks and I'm tired of it. I'm being honest, not mean.

Ms. Carter gives the slightest of smiles as she looks at the poster under my arm. "You do understand, Blythe, you have to have passing grades to enjoy any extracurricular activities in this school. I appreciate that you have used your time off to make up some of your schoolwork, but that does not change your grade in here. As far as I have seen, your grades are still not high enough for club participation. Even if you do have a certain teacher who seems to have made you his class pet." Her faint smile drops as the bell rings and she shushes me to my seat.

"Class, please open your books to page seventy-nine. Ms. Tanner is going to teach us this next concept. Ms. Tanner, you will receive ten extra credit points if you are able to teach it well. It will not make a dent in your poor performance, but it is the thought that counts."

Right, her thoughts are so generous.

I sigh, knowing there's nothing I can do about it. As my dad said, sometimes we have people in our lives who won't give us a chance, or who treat us poorly. We may not be able to remove them from our lives, but if we're smart and kind, we can figure out how to get along with them.

I'm going to have to learn to get along with her and I may as well get started. I put my poster down, swallow the knowledge that I won't be able to enter the contest, and head to the board with the best smile I can manage.

I face the board with the book in my hand, turned to page seventy-nine. I glance down at the page to make sure I know what I'm supposed to teach. My mind whirls with wondering where to start. The bubbles in my stomach feel much lighter than the lying bubbles felt, but they're still uncomfortable.

Balancing the book in my one hand and trying to write with the other, and also teach, feels like too many things to do at once, so I slam the book closed and set it down.

Ms. Carter gives me a wide-eyed stare and looks like she wants to slam me. But she settles back down with a small smile. Probably waiting for me to fail.

I won't let that happen.

I turn to the class and take a deep breath.

Marsha gives me a "you-can-do-it" smile, and it's just what I need.

"Okay. We've dealt with solving for X before, right?" I look at the class to make sure they're listening.

I see some nods, but most of the people look bored. Marsha still smiles at me.

"And we've done number lines before, right?

One kid yawns. Maybe teaching isn't my thing. But I've got to prove to Ms. Carter that I can do it. I don't care as much about the ten points, as I want her to know I'm good at some things.

A tune, My Favorite Things, from The Sound of Music comes into my head and I run with it, singing a verse with my own words.

> X is the number that we want to solve for.
> Stuck by itself we will then know our answer.
> How do we get it alone by itself?
> These are the steps that we take to get there.

It didn't rhyme, but everyone was looking at me. Not one bored face. Marsha looked like she was holding back a giggle. I didn't dare look at the teacher.

"Let's go to the problem on the board." I point to what Ms. Carter has written. "How do we get X stuck by itself?" I ask.

A couple of hands shoot up. It doesn't take long for us to have that part of the problem solved.

Then we go to the other half of the problem. This part might be harder for them. Not because it's really hard, but because it's different. Sometimes when things are different, we freeze up. We think more about how it's different than about how some of it is the same as something we've done before.

Like me this year in school. I froze up when things got hard, and by freezing up, my brain couldn't come up with the answers about how to solve my problem. So I grabbed on to the easy, but wrong answer of cheating.

I take a deep breath and move over to the number line. The numbers are already written in. We just have to figure out where to put X.

"So," I say, pointing to the number line. "We know that

X is more than thirty-two. How do we show that on a number line?"

Silence.

Dead silence.

I give them a little longer, getting more and more uncomfortable. I can give them the answer, but it feels like it should come from them. Kids start squirming in their seats and I hear Ms. Carter clearing her throat. I'm about to answer it myself and have begun turning to the board when I see a hand shoot up from the corner of my eye.

Marsha.

Marsha is trying to save me.

Again.

She hasn't raised her hand in class all year, and every time I've seen her get called on, she speaks so softly that even sitting near her, I can't hear what she says. Will she know the answer? If she gets it wrong, will that make her miserable? I'm not sure what to do, but she starts waving her hand around like I can't see it and that's when I know everything will be okay.

"Marsha?" I ask. "Would you like to come up to the board and show us what to do?"

She nods, turning kind of pink, then stands and walks up next to me. She gives me her shy smile, but grabs the chalk like a champ and draws a line to the right, above and just to the right of the 32. Then she puts down the chalk, turns to me, smiles a giant smile, and heads back to her seat.

She did it! She faced her fears and saved me from being embarrassed.

I'm so happy I complimented her fabric in sewing class and helped her with her books and papers that day when I knocked them over.

I grab the chalk and finish the problem. "If you look in your book, you can see that they put a circle around 32 to show that the answer starts just past the whole number." I add a circle to the front of the line.

"Any questions?"

Nope?

Ten points to me!

As I go back to my seat, Marsha beams and silent claps for me. I sigh as I sit, but it's a good sigh, and when Marsha glances over, I give her thumbs up.

Chapter 60
Tuesday, After School

The Decision

I run to Mr. Scott's classroom as fast as I can. With this being a special club day for most of the clubs, the buses will bring us home, which means the club will be crowded. My fingers and toes are crossed (very uncomfortable in shoes), hoping I've brought my grades up enough to officially join the club and enter the contest. After class with Ms. Carter, I don't have anything but a spoonful of hope. Maybe someone hadn't yet put in all of my scores from the later work I'd turned in.

My poster with my entry is tucked under my arm. I've kept it with me all day, afraid to let it out of my sight. The corner is a bit bent, but overall it still looks good.

There are a couple of students at Mr. Scott's desk talking to him, so I do my best to be patient. The new medicine I'm taking has mostly worn off, so I'm kind of antsy, as well as hungry, but I stand there as still as I can.

Just before it's my turn, he stands. "Please sit down. Let's get started. How many of you have an entry for the contest?"

Quite a few kids raise their hands. I find an empty chair

near the back of the room and pull a granola bar from my lunch bag.

"I'll see you one at a time at my desk. We'll make sure you've followed all the rules and get your entry recorded. Then you may leave or wait here for the buses. Alphabetical order. James Atwater?"

As James goes to the front I sigh. It'll take a long time to get to Tanner. I get out a notebook and start doodling.

"Bly Tanner," Mr. Scott calls.

My medicine must still be working a bit because I hear him. I close my notebook, pick up my poster, and hurry to the front of the room.

"Hi, Bly, what have you got there?" He asks, pointing to my poster.

"My entry," I say, showing it to him.

"'We are > the Sum of Our Parts,' I like the theme," he says, his eyes looking over the photos. "These are great, and they show the theme really well. Is that your sister?" He points to Sarah trying to skip. "I love the look of concentration on her face."

"Yeah. Her name is Sarah. She was trying to skip." I look at my little sister with new eyes. She's trying so hard at something and can't quite do it by herself. After the picture, I'd helped her and she almost had it. All she needed was a little bit of help.

Like me. A little bit of help from my parents, believing in me and setting up a homework time, a little bit of help from my teachers, which Ms. Bowers says is coming, and a little bit of help from some medicine, which I hope I won't have to take for long. Maybe long enough to learn some other coping skills. Positive ones.

"Sarah gave me the idea for the theme," I say, as he hands me the poster.

"This is great work," he says, "but we have two problems."

I sigh. "I know. My grades aren't up enough," I say as I turn to leave.

"Wait, Bly. I have more to say."

I turn back to him trying not to let him see how wet my eyes are getting.

He reaches for the poster and I let him spread it out on his desk. "How long have you been taking pictures?" he asks.

"Since I got a camera in August," I say. I reach for the poster, beginning to feel possessive of it.

But he raises his hand, stopping me. "Like I said, these are good. And printed with Instapic film, which means you haven't done any editing."

"Of course not. You can't edit them. They shoot right out of the camera." I wonder what he's getting at.

"May I please see your camera, Bly?" Mr. Scott asks.

I run to my desk and bring Polly back to show him.

"This isn't bad. It takes nice pictures," He says, turning Polly around in his hands. "And, look, they're downloadable."

"What?" I grab the camera and look to where he's pointing. There's a computer port.

"Did it come with a cord?"

"Yes," I say, "but I thought that was to charge the battery."

207

I take the camera, jumping up and down with excitement. "I don't always have to use the expensive film!"

"And speaking of that," Mr. Scott says, "entries are to be submitted online. That's the something else I wanted to tell you."

"Oh," I say. I look around the room. For the first time, I notice that no one else is carrying around a poster with pictures. "Um, oops? Can I blame it on ADHD?" I ask, giggling.

"Speaking of that," he says. "You got tested?"

I look around to make sure no one is listening. I nod and half-smile. "Yeah."

"I know it probably feels strange to have a diagnosis like that, but here, see if this helps a bit." He opens his bottom desk drawer and hands me a piece of paper. "Here's a list of some famous people that may have had learning disabilities, maybe even ADHD."

I take the paper and my poster and turn again to leave.

"One more thing, Bly."

I turn back once more.

"May I keep the poster until next week? I think it'll be a great example to show the club about following a theme."

It only takes a second of thought. "Yeah, that'd be great."

Chapter 61
Wednesday, Bus Ride Home

Double Selfie

When Cherie gets on the bus, I glance up. She looks perfect, as usual, in skinny jeans and an argyle sweater. A quick glance at her nails shows me she's trimmed them short and polished them. She gives me a slight nod of the head when she passes. Does that mean she's forgiven me for turning her in?

Before I can stop myself, I'm racing down the aisle to Cherie.

"No changing seats while the bus is moving, Fly girl," Asteroid shouts.

"Sorry, Asteroid," I yell back, slipping into the empty seat next to Cherie.

"What?" Cherie doesn't look up from the doodle she's drawing.

"I wanna ask you about this, you know, this. . . ." I hesitate.

Cherie stops doodling and turns towards me. "What?"

I can't figure out her tone. It isn't exactly mad or mean,

but it isn't friendly either. I take a deep breath and try to speak. "Did you," I stop and take a breath. "Did you, are you still upset about. . . ."

Cherie sticks her pen in the spirals of her notebook and stares at me. "What do you think? I'm grounded for life and suspended from Cheer."

"Oh," I say. I lean back and look up at the ceiling. There's a spit wad hanging on the roof of the bus over the guy in front of me.

Do I regret telling on us? I think for a minute.

No, I don't. I no longer have that icky feeling in the pit of my stomach. I don't have to remember all the lies to keep myself out of trouble. And I'm finally getting some help so I can be the smart person in school I know I am.

Did she have anything good come from it? I have to ask. "Have you, um, figured out about your," I'm not sure how to say it. I blurt it out, "Your problem with writing?"

Cherie stays quiet so I sit still and wait. Then she speaks so softly, for a second, I'm not sure I hear her. "You knew?"

I nod. "I figured it out after you gave me that note."

She sighs and schooches down in her seat. The only other time I've seen her look so down is when she left the parent-teacher meeting before mine started. "I have to go to resource while they figure out how to help me. Dad says I'm just stupid and don't try, but the resource teacher says I have dyslexia." She glances at me. "I don't know why I'm telling you this."

I dig into my backpack for the paper from Mr. Scott.

"You're not stupid," I say, as I keep looking for the paper. "Remember how you thought of new groupings in science class, groupings even Porter hadn't thought of? And remember how you recited your entire report on your fridge to me. I just wrote it. You got an A. I didn't even turn one in."

Her eyes bore into me. "What? You didn't turn one in?"

I pull out the paper from Mr. Scott and hand it to her. "I wanted your help with cheating because I was doing really bad. I keep forgetting things and losing things and, well, never mind, that would take too long to tell you how I've messed up. But I found out I've got ADHD. And look, Mr. Scott gave me this. You can have it."

She takes the paper from me as if I'm holding a bug she isn't sure she wants to touch. It has pictures of famous people like Einstein. I figure even if she can't read well, she can probably recognize the pictures.

"These are famous people that may have had learning problems. Like us. Look, Einstein." I point to the guy with the messy hair.

"He looks like Mr. Bines," she says, a giggle escaping.

"That's what I think," I say.

She scans the page. "That's Melody Sallyforth, from 'Rescue Miami,'" she says, pointing to a woman near the bottom.

I read what it says. "She has dyslexia. See, it's like science class. The classification system. If we're gonna classify ourselves, we can't call ourselves stupid. That's a misclassification."

Cherie's eyes light up. "Melody Sallyforth? Seriously?"

She uses her finger on the description below the picture and must figure out enough because she looks at me with the brightest smile I've ever seen on her. It's a real smile, not the plastered one she uses when she pretends she's being nice. She screams and gives me a hug. "We're misclassified!"

"Um, okay," I say, stunned. Then my eyes get big with a new idea. I pull out Polly. "Will you take a picture with me? I want to add it to my themed pictures."

"Your what?" Cherie gives me the stinking garbage look, but I plow through and repeat myself.

"My 'We are > the Sum of Our parts' pictures. We're perfect how we are, even with our imperfections. In fact, "I say, a new thought coming to me. "We are perfect because of our imperfections."

"I'm not sure that makes sense," Cherie says.

I shrug my shoulders. "Maybe not, but it sounds good."

We pose together and I take a selfie with Polly, Cherie and me with our heads together smiling. Who'd have ever thought that would happen?

There's just enough time for the picture to develop before Cherie has to get off at her stop.

"Don't post it anywhere. And, this doesn't change things between us," she says, staring at me in warning as she gets up from her seat.

"For my eyes only," I say.

And the picture?

It's perfect.

Chapter 62

P.S. Q&A

Q: What is black and white and blue all over?

A: Dad in a tux and me in my first formal dress—blue with grey squiggles.

Q: Who got Jennifer Gardoney's autograph?

A: Me, of course, silly! No one said you couldn't go with your family.

Q: Who got a sip of sparkling, pink, non-alcoholic champagne?

A: Me, again! It tickled my nose.

Q: Who entered and won the contest?

A: I don't know. Some kid from West Chicago. But Chester, the Pyrenees dog guy, got an Honorable Mention and I clapped louder than everyone!

Q: When might Ms. Gardoney come back to Chicago?

A: It was such a success, she's coming back next year!!

Author's Note

Neurodiversity has become a buzz word, but hopefully talking about it will lead to more individualized help for children caught in a school system that is set up for the average learner. Obviously this is difficult to achieve in oversized and underfunded classes with underpaid teachers. Awareness of the challenges these kids have is a first step.

Many children given the diagnoses of ADHD are put on medication. While this isn't the answer for everyone, and can be controversial, it may help children get to a point where they can pay attention enough to learn some coping skills that build as they grow. As a doctor once told me – you wouldn't deny a child with a broken leg a pair of crutches.

You can find all sorts of information about ADHD – from blaming it on sugar consumption and bad parenting, to those denying the condition, all the way to those saying ADHD is a gift in strange packaging. If you want an overview, I would suggest going to chadd.org as a first step.

Acknowledgments

This is the book that taught me how to write a novel. Many people helped polish it over time, so I ask forgiveness for names not listed.

The WIFYR conference led by Carol Lynch Williams has been an invaluable resource for growing my writing skills in general and this manuscript in particular. Laura Torres Newey, Claudia Mills, Tim Wynn-Jones, Martine Leavitt, J. Scott Savage, and Stephen Fraser were all great workshop mentors.

Carol Lynch Williams and Becky Barnes for telling me things that turned on important light bulbs in my mind.

My many beta readers and critique group members. Here's where I'm going to miss the most names. Melva Gifford, Deanna Adamson, Lana Krumwiede, Amy Smith, Ceil Young, Karen Peck, Heather Bullough, Michelle Ernst, Michelle and Jenny Hubbard. All of you have helped strengthen the manuscript and give much needed encouragement.

I also need to thank those who verified things for me. Matthew Kirby for his help with ADHD diagnoses. Olivia Mohlman and Sophie Child for checking my math for accuracy and age appropriateness. Any mistakes left with either are the mistakes of the author.

Thank you to Chicken Scratch Books and Kiri Jorgensen for falling in love with the story and making it even better with their vision

And, always, thank you to my family for cheering me on and not complaining when I forgot to cook dinner.

About The Author

Susan Phelan

When Susan was in Junior High, she announced that she was going to be an actress. She eventually did become a professional actress, but before that, she rode horses, raised five children and several guide dog puppies, nursed a zoo of assorted animals, and worked (if you could use that term) in a library. Somewhere in the midst of wrestling kids and animals, she took up writing, because, as she puts it, life is made up of stories. When she's not acting in stories or telling stories, Susan likes to play with her family and make messes in the kitchen, or any other flat surface she can find.

Chicken Scratch Reading School
Miss Classified – **Novel Study Courses**
www.chickenscratchbooks.com/courses

Join us at **Chicken Scratch Reading School** for your choice of 2 different online Novel Study Courses for *Miss Classified*. Created by certified teachers with extensive curriculum design experience, these offerings are 4 or 6-week courses of study for 5th- 8th grade students. They include reading study focus, interviews, quizzes, vocabulary work, thematic and character analysis, a written essay, and culmination project. The courses include a mix of online and on-paper work, highlighted by instructional **videos** from the author, Susan Phelan, and publisher Kiri Jorgensen.

Chicken Scratch Books creates online novel study courses for every book we publish.
Our goal is to teach our readers to appreciate strong new traditional literature.

At Chicken Scratch Books,
Traditional Literature is all we do.

We Fill the Gap

Mainstream and Religious
Children's Book Publishers
used to run side-by-side.

Now they've split

Mainstream Publishers

Religious Publishers